FLASHPOINT

AN ALEX MASON THRILLER

DAVID ARCHER

BLAKE BANNER

RIGHTHOUSE

ISBN-13: 978-1-63696-151-4

ISBN-10: 1-63696-151-7

Cover design by: Damonza

Printed in the United States of America

www.righthouse.com

www.instagram.com/righthousebooks

www.facebook.com/righthousebooks

twitter.com/righthousebooks

PRAISE FOR ALEX MASON

"It is brutal, wastes no time, and is full of action."

"Better than Bond, Bourne, or Reacher."

"For fans of Clancy, Mitch App, and Brad Taylor."

"Same level as Patterson or Baldacci."

"This book is filled with action, intrigue, espionage, and everything else lovers of a good thriller want."

ALEX MASON THRILLERS

PROLOGUE

THE HEAT WAS HEAVY UNDER A MOLTEN SUN. IT
didn't sparkle on the Atlantic Ocean. It lay like an incandes-
cent sheet of steel, blinding to look at and obscuring the
waves beneath its glare, in the Gulf of Cadiz. A group of
men stood clustered around an apparently haphazard collec-
tion of machines. Some were mounted on trucks, Land
Rovers and Jeeps. Others were set on the ground and had
cables, like tendrils, stretching out across the wild scrubland
of the Coto Doñana nature reserve. Along the cables were
sensors that probed deep into the ground beneath the nature
reserve, deep into the very bowels of the Earth.

The technology was cutting edge, more advanced than
anything in Europe or the States. It was the result of millions
of dollars of investment in research and development in
particle physics resonance; and it had been developed specifi-
cally for this one job: to find crude oil deposits deep under-
ground in Andalusia, in the south of Spain.

And it had been developed, in absolute secrecy, by

Russian laboratories subcontracted to the Russian Department of Advanced Research, which was in turn a sub-department of the Office for Innovative Design and Development, a branch of the top-secret Russian Research Institute at Tver.

It was one of several projects stretching across the autonomous region of Andalusia, from the deserts of Almeria and Granada in the east, through the sedimentary rock formations of the mountains of Malaga and eastern Cadiz, right across to the flats of the Atlantic coast of Cadiz and Huelva.

Dr. Jose Carlos Montilla was the head of the project. He had the data in from Almeria and Granada, he had just received the data from the mountains of Malaga, and now he was reading the data coming back from the sensors across the coast of Cadiz and Huelva. As he read it he sent it to print and ran across the flats back toward his field office. His belly was on fire and his head was reeling.

He burst through the cabin door. His assistant was at the computer and looked around as he came in. He snapped, "Out! Go! Go!"

She scuttled out and he slammed the door, sat and picked up the telephone that gave him a secure line to the office of Benjamin Musa in Seville, at his office in the Palace of San Telmo, the seat of the Junta de Andalucia, the Andalusian autonomous executive. Benjamin Musa was a powerful man. He was the head of the Andalusian Socialist Party and the leader of the opposition. He had risen to his position of power through a subtle use of bribery, and where that had failed, blackmail. He owned Montilla both because he had proof of the latter's use of drugs—which he himself had provided for him—and because he now provided him with a thousand euros a month as a supplement to his salary; a thousand euros on which Montilla had become completely dependent.

Musa snatched up the telephone.

"Yes!"

"Benjamin, I have all the data in. You will not believe this. Are you alone?"

"Yes. Tell me."

"There are deep oil reserves running from beneath the Mediterranean coast of Almeria right across Andalusia and out into the Gulf of Cadiz. As far as I can tell it reaches out into the Alboran Sea. It is *vast*. I have never seen anything like it."

Benjamin Musa laughed. "Oh, that is good, Jose Carlos, that is very good. I need your report on my desk by this evening. Absolutely *nobody* must get this information but me. Get on it now, not a word to anyone."

Jose Carlos hesitated. "Benjamin, I have done what you wanted. You will now release me?"

"Yes, Jose Carlos, of course I will. A promise is a promise. But let's not waste time. Put that report together and get it to me before six PM. And you will be a free man."

Benjamin Musa put down the phone and sat a moment gazing at the bright sunshine beyond his triple-glazed window. He watched the giant pine tree by the river on the Paseo de las Delicias, swaying in total silence. He looked at the London plane trees on the Paseo de Roma. He smiled. Achieving this corner office had been a triumph. What he was going to do now would dwarf anything he had achieved in the past.

He opened a drawer and extracted the secure, dedicated phone he had there, and dialed a number in Moscow. And two thousand five hundred miles away, to the north and east, Colonel Alexandrina Vitsin picked up her receiver and took her time putting it to her ear, as she exhaled smoke through her nose.

"Yes, Musa."

"The results are in. The report will be on my desk by six this evening, eight PM your time."

"Good. What steps will you take?"

"I will make a statement outside the Parliament here in Seville—"

"No."

She could almost hear him frown. "No?"

"Madrid. Palacio de la Cortes, on the steps of your parliament. Alert the press that you plan to make a statement. CNN, BBC, Reuters, everybody. Next week."

He nodded. "Yes, yes OK. I'll let you know when it's arranged."

She didn't answer. She hung up.

Benjamin Musa sat looking at the phone for a moment, chewing his lip. He had never met the colonel, but he had a mental image of what she looked like. He had often fantasized about slapping her violently. Now he sighed and put the thought aside. He dialed another number, in Seville. It rang twice and a raw voice made rough by unfiltered cigarettes and cognac said, "What?"

"Tonight. Steal a car. Make it look like a hit and run, or a mugging..."

"Don't tell me how to do my job. The price went up." A

cruel smile in the voice. "I know how important this is to you."

"How much?"

"Twenty K."

Quique was a gypsy. He was the one guy he had never been able to blackmail. Gypsies were all about family and closing ranks, honor and pride. If he had Quique killed, he would soon follow him to the grave. And if he stopped using him, they would destroy him. He would have to deal with them sooner or later. But not yet.

"OK, twenty thousand, but Quique?"

"What is it, Benny?"

"Don't push too far. Even you have a limit."

"Sure, you just tell me when I get there."

His laugh was like sawing wood. Musa hung up and looked at the silent, waving trees again. By six he would have his report, by ten the loose end of Jose Carlos would be tied up; and early next week he would light the fuse under the biggest crisis Europe had seen since Hitler invaded Poland on September 3rd, 1939.

ONE

On Tuesday, 5th September, at ten o'clock in the morning, the camera crews, photographers and reporters began to gather on the sidewalk outside the Congress on the Plaza de los Palacios. There were three police riot vans placed strategically around the square. Thirteen steps rose from the sidewalk to the six Greco-Roman columns that held the Palladian portico. At the top, in front of the massive oak doors two cops in balaclavas stood with assault rifles. The doors were open and four more armed guards stood inside.

By ten thirty the sidewalk was jammed with people. Several news anchors were speaking to cameras, while crowds gathered either side of the road, waiting to see what was going to happen. The CNN anchor was saying, "Madrid is rife with gossip, but it seems nobody knows for sure, Alysin, what is going to happen today. Benjamin Musa, the controversial leader of the Andalusian Socialist Party, leader of the opposition in the autonomous community of Andalusia, has stated that he will make a statement to the nation here, on the steps of Congress, this morning shortly before eleven o'clock. Like I said, nobody is sure what the statement is about, but there are rumors that it will involve a greater independence of Andalusia from Madrid..."

He paused and looked to where a black limousine was pulling up opposite the steps.

"I think this may be him now—"

As he spoke the doors opened and three men got out. Two were in dark suits and one was dressed in a blue blazer with an open shirt and chinos. He held a folder in his hand. The two suits closed in on him and he strode through the crowd toward the steps, one of them either side. He climbed seven of the thirteen steps, stopped and turned. Behind and above him, four cops with assault rifles emerged from the palace, fanned out and stood looking down at the crowd.

The camera crews closed in, swarming up the stairs to surround him, while a cluster of microphones bristled in front of him. Benjamin Musa gazed out at the crowd.

"Andalusia!" He almost yelled the word. "Andalusia, for five thousand years or more, Andalusia was the heart of the Iberian peninsula. From legendary Tartesos, the most powerful city on the Atlantic, to Cordoba, the second city of the Roman empire, Cordoba again as the Light of the West, the seat of the Caliphs, the most powerful city in Europe.

"But now we are the agricultural backwater of Spain, exploited by Madrid, by Catalonia, by the Basque Country, exploited by tourists and expatriates from all over Europe, exploited by Brussels. Today, we are a shadow of our former glory."

He nodded, looking at the journalists, at the cameras, one by one.

"Until now," he said. "Today, I bring news to the people of Spain, I bring news to the Congress, and I bring news *for* the people of Andalusia. Our servitude in Spain, and in the European Union is finished. Today, we rise again to our former glory. Today, the proud people of Andalusia rise up and say, 'Enough!'"

He held up the folder for all to see and raised his voice.

"I hold here a report. A report which I have commissioned in secret, because I know the nefarious forces which are at work in this building behind me. Forces that would suppress this report and bury it, to keep the Andalusian people under the Spanish yoke. But this report proves beyond any doubt that Andalusia rests on one of the biggest reserves of crude oil in the world. Andalusia is rich! And it is time we honored our heritage and took our place among the great, oil-rich nations of the Mediterranean. Listen to me, and listen carefully. This is not Spanish oil, this is not European oil, this is Andalusian oil. Spain, Brussels, you want our oil? *Os den por culo!* You can come and make a line and buy it!"

With that he turned and ran up the remaining six steps with his bodyguards at his side, and disappeared into the parliamentary building.

TWO

THE PHONE WAS RINGING AND I COULD NOT breathe. I opened my eyes. Everything was pitch black and somebody was pushing a cushion down on my face. My lungs were screaming for air. The phone rang violently. I lurched and sat up, clawing at my face. Manny Pacquiao, my obnoxious cat, took a swipe at me and dropped off the bed.

I grabbed at the phone on my bedside table and spoke with difficulty.

"Yeah."

"Did you see it?"

I leaned back against the pillows and rolled my eyes.

"Sir, it's five in the morning. All I have seen is my cat's furry underbelly while he tried to suffocate me."

"Your facetiousness is inappropriate at the moment, Mason. Be in my office in half an hour. Don't shower. It takes too long."

I hung up and Manny Pacquiao leered at me from the top of the wardrobe as I made my way to the shower.

Thirty-five minutes later I was buzzed into Nero's office on Wilson Boulevard, in Rosslyn. He had what you could only describe as baleful eyes and he watched me with them as I sat down.

"Well?" he asked me.

"Well, what, sir?"

"Did you see it, confound it!"

"I told you, all I saw was my cat's belly. I was asleep. Most people are asleep at five AM, sir."

"Ridiculous." He pressed a button on his desk. A female voice said, "Yes, sir?"

"Coffee. Croissants. Is Lovelock there?"

"No sir, she's at home. This is Joyce."

"Good grief! Joyce?" He said it like he didn't believe anyone was really called Joyce. "Coffee, fresh butter croissants, fresh cream, butter. Lovelock knows..."

"Yes sir."

He released the button, looked at me and drew breath. I said, "I didn't see it, sir. I still don't know what 'it' is."

"You were not alerted by contacts in the press that an event was brewing in Spain this morning?"

"No, sir. Does this mean I don't get breakfast?" He stared at me until I realized I had asked the wrong question. "What happened in Madrid, sir?"

"Benjamin Musa, the leader of the socialist opposition in the Andalusian parliament, has called for Andalusian independence."

I looked at the window behind his head, where the horizon was turning a translucent gray-blue, and wondered whether the glass was bulletproof.

"I am not well up on Spanish politics, sir, but I seem to

remember Catalonia declared independence a few years back, the Basques had a long tradition of bombing their way to freedom, they had a civil war in '36 before which all the parliamentarians used to scream death threats at each other across the chamber."

"Your point?"

"I think it's the Mediterranean temperament. They are genetically predisposed to threaten to kill each other and declare independence. The Italians do it to."

The door opened and a nice lady in a blue cardigan came in with a large tray of croissants, coffee, butter and cream. She set it on the desk, smiled at us in order of relative importance and said, "There you are, dears. If you need anything, just shout."

When the door had closed he said, "Joyce," thoughtfully before pouring coffee.

"Spain is a prominent member of the European Union. It is composed of autonomous regions, each with its own parliament and executive, rather like a federation. Spain is potentially a rich country, but if the communities split apart, Spain's economy would collapse. Andalusia is a huge source of revenue, from tourism, shipping and not least, olive oil. If Andalusia seceded, Spain would become bankrupt."

I was stuffing a croissant into my mouth and held up two fingers.

"One, what's it to us, and two, surely the people of Andalusia would not be that stupid. They need Spain as much as Spain needs them."

"That was true, Alex, but it seems Benjamin Musa commissioned a secret report into deep-lying crude oil deposits beneath Andalusia. Spain's oil deposits have always been considered negligible, though its geology seemed promising. This report reveals, however, that the cavities that held the oil beneath the surface collapsed when the sierras were formed—quite recently in geological time—and the oil reserves drained down to a lower, more inaccessible level. This is important for two reasons."

He stuffed a croissant into his mouth and chewed, watching me. I knew this was my cue to sound intelligent.

"The technology," I said and he nodded. I went on. "The technology to produce this report didn't exist, so where did Musa get the technology?"

"To produce the report and extract the oil."

"OK, and..."

"The only people who have that technology, and it is truly cutting edge, are the Russians. While the West has been gearing up to phase out oil, Russia has been developing extraordinarily sophisticated equipment to find and exploit deep deposits."

"Oh." I nodded slowly as the implications began to dawn on me. "So the Russians have supplied the leader of the Andalusian socialist opposition with a plausible motive to declare independence and promise the people of Andalusia the kind of prosperity they can only dream of today,"

"While shouting about Madrid and Brussels stealing their wealth."

"This is revenge for Ukraine. They are putting a Russian puppet state—not on NATO's doorstep, right inside the door."

"We need to know how far Russia is prepared to go, how far Musa is prepared to go—"

"And perhaps more to the point," I interrupted, "how far Madrid is prepared to go."

"I was coming to that. Musa made his declaration just over an hour ago, and there is apparently a furious debate going on right now inside the parliamentary chamber in Congress. But there are some worrying features to this, Alex. The first is Musa's language. He has always made a thing of Andalusia's Mediterranean heritage, but lately, and today in particular, he has been stressing Andalusia's Arab past. Cordoba, in Southern Spain, was a powerful empire under the Ummayad caliphs. It sounds as though he is making overtures to his Arab and North African neighbors to form some kind of alliance."

"That brings Islam as well as oil into the mix."

"Precisely. The Arab nations have long considered Al-andalus—Andalusia to us—to be an Arab state, robbed from them by the Spanish. Now, if this posturing slides into civil unrest, or indeed civil war, and a foreign nation should lend Andalusia support, either overtly or covertly—remember, we are talking about some of the richest oil reserves on the planet, a prize worth risking war for..."

I finished for him. "Madrid could call on its NATO allies and we could see war in Europe for the first time in eighty years."

"So the question is, as you said, how far are the parties prepared to go? The prize is enormous. I fear they will be prepared to go all the way." He heaved a huge sigh that ended as a big grunt. "Twice since Vietnam, the CIA has lured Russia into wars that have all but crippled her economically. Afghanistan ultimately caused the collapse of the Soviet Union, along with a few other contributing factors.

This was a deliberate strategy by the Central Intelligence Agency. But now it seems someone in Moscow has very skillfully turned the tables on us, and unless we can pull something very clever out of our hat, I see us on a slippery slide, headed for a very costly, destructive war in Europe."

"What do you want me to do?"

"I don't know, but you had better be ready to travel to Spain at short notice. With a bit of luck all this posturing will resolve itself into the European Council and Madrid giving Andalusia—and Benjamin Musa—some kind of privileged position, and his backing off from the brink of war. We'll see what comes out of this meeting of the Congress today. The Spanish president is due to make a statement late this afternoon." The eyebrow he arched at me was as baleful as the dark eye beneath it. "You might try to watch it."

"I will." I nodded. "I will try to watch it."

I left and as I passed through the antechamber where Lovelock usually sat, I found Joyce in her blue cardigan. She was sewing a button onto a huge pair of pants. She smiled and I frowned.

"Are those...?"

"Mm-hmm."

"Does he know...?"

She shook her head and looked oddly satisfied. "I've been with him for years. He has no idea."

I rode the elevator down to the parking garage reflecting on the fact that it is often that which is most obviously in front of our noses that we are least aware of. Manny Pacquiao lying on my face, the Russians searching for oil in southern Spain, a woman in your house whose been stitching your pants for the last ten years and you don't know she's there. These are the things that can kill you, and you're just not aware of them.

I drove home in my TVR Griffith and started packing a suitcase. At eight I went down to the kitchen and made a proper breakfast of bacon, eggs, toast and sausages, along with a pint of espresso coffee, and sat watching the news while I ate.

They were already calling it the Spanish Crisis. Some guy on the BBC tried to coin "Spaxit," but I didn't think that was going to catch on. Besides sounding like a mental condition, it didn't cover the issue by a long shot. This wasn't just Spain following Britain back to independence from the Euro-Empire. This was Spain disintegrating like all the glue was melting.

After rehashing the basics, CNN cut to footage taken inside the Spanish Parliament, where Jesus Sanchez, the leader of the right wing Popular Party, and the president of the Spanish government, was making a statement. Over there it was apparently three PM lunchtime in the Med, and everyone would be glued to their TVs.

He was surprisingly young. He made his way to the lectern in a dark-blue suit with an open shirt. Obviously ties were not the big thing in Spain. I find it hard to vote for any politician, but a politician without a tie? That's like somebody saying to you, "I'm going to sit here for four years and get paid a lot of money for doing pretty much nothing—and I am not even going to *pretend* to be serious about my job."

I don't know if Jesius Sanchez was serious or if he was putting on a show, but whatever it was, it was convincing. His face was taut and there was real anger in his eyes. As he started talking the voice of a simultaneous interpreter kicked in over the top on the TV.

"We have heard a lot in recent months, weeks and days, about the glorious heritage of Andalusia, the Caliphs of Cordoba, the eight hundred years during which Andalusia was not occupied by the Arabs, but during which Al-andalus was a shining light of Arab culture in Europe. Eight-hundred-years."

He leaned on the dispatch box, nodding, looking around at the congressmen and women. Then he leaned forward and spoke like he was fighting to control his anger.

"Fourteen hundred and ninety-two! Over five hundred and thirty years ago, the last Arabs were expelled from Granada! I would like to ask Mr. Musa, how many years does Andalusia have to be integrated within Spain before it becomes Spanish! A thousand years? Two thousand years?"

He paused, looking around again. He was not reading from notes. This was spontaneous and he meant it.

"I would say to Mr. Musa, and to *all* Spaniards, that integration does not come from years of domination, but from integration. And I will tell this house and this nation *right now* that no part of Spain is more intimately identified with Spanish culture and Spanish identity than Andalusia. What could be more Spanish than flamenco, the Giralda of Seville, the cathedral of Cordoba or the Alhambra of Granada? Andalusia is at the heart of the Spanish soul, and to deny that Andalusia is Spanish is to deny that Spain exists at all!"

Another pause and he actually wiped tears from his eyes.

"So why? Why is Mr. Musa engaging in this attempt against the integrity of the kingdom? Why, when Spain is finally prospering in democratic union with the wider Europe, when we are finally emerging from the economic crises that have hurt us so badly as a nation, why does he now seek to destroy our homeland and our kingdom?" He nodded. "I will tell you."

He poured water from a decanter and sipped.

"I will tell you: because he is hungry for the power that he thinks will come to him from an independent, oil-rich Andalusia, because he is blinded by his own greed, because he does not see the economic crisis that he will precipitate and the poverty and hardship he will bring down upon his own people, because he is *blind* to the inevitable imposition of Islam on Andalusia as a precondition to his joining this famous 'Mediterranean Club' of oil-rich countries. But above all, ladies, gentlemen, people of Spain, because he does not *care*, just so long as he can exercise personal control over that oil."

He paused again and stood, leaning on the dispatch box, staring down at the space between his hands. When he looked up, his face was tight, pale, drawn with anger.

"But if I give you the impression that I am asking Mr. Musa to desist and withdraw his demand for independence, then forgive me. Because I have not expressed myself correctly. Let me be clear. The oil beneath Andalusia does not belong to Andalusia any more than the fish from Galicia belongs to Galicia or the steel from the Basque Country belongs to the Basques. That oil belongs to the Spanish people, and if—*if*—a decision is taken *by the Spanish government* to exploit that oil, then it will be done for the benefit of Spain.

"And let me make a final couple of points: there will be

no referendum on the independence of Andalusia, there will be no parliamentary debate on the subject, and if Mr. Musa persists in his attempts to destroy the union of the Kingdom, he faces trial for treason. We, in this house, must be tireless in protecting the integrity of Spain, and the benefit of *all* the Spanish people. *Viva España!*"

There was a lot of applause. My own feeling was that he'd done a good job, and I could imagine that all eyes in the European Commission and the European Council must have been glued on him. Right now it was a storm in a teacup. But if Musa was the right—or more accurately, the *wrong* kind of man, this could turn into a major constitutional crisis, or worse. After all, as Nero had said, we were not dealing with carrots, or even wheat, we were dealing with some of the largest oil reserves on the planet, at a time when oil was running out and there was still no credible alternative.

THREE

Jesus Sanchez was in the back of his dark blue Audi S8, watching the lights of Madrid slip by in the night. Beside him was Alvaro Romero, the man who had been his ally and friend for the last fifteen years. Romero watched the president—the president he had created—and saw the anxiety ill concealed on his face.

"This will blow over," he told him. "Just as Tejero's coup blew over, just as Catalan independence blew over. Social progress is a relentless force, Jesus. It is like gravity, it draws us ever closer to the center. First it was Rome, then it was the Vatican, then it was London, Washington DC, now it is Brussels."

Jesus flicked his eyes at him. "Philosophy, Alvaro. This is not a time for philosophy. This is a pragmatic problem."

"That's what I am trying to tell you." He paused, watched the light and shadow from the streetlamps wash over his friend's face. "You must been seen to be reacting energetically, appeal to the people, enlist the support of the king, but be confident. Benjamin has no hope of success. This play of his is childish."

They pulled onto the Gran Via and moved toward the Carretera de la Princesa. The leaves of the plane trees mottled the light from the streetlamps. Sanchez watched the subway stations slip by. The shops were open still. They wouldn't close till nine or nine thirty, and people swarmed on the sidewalks, lightly dressed for the heat.

Jesus turned to study his friend's face. "Putin's invasion of Chechnya was childish, but childish men hungry for power do childish, reckless things. I have known Benjamin for many years. He tried to blackmail me—"

"I remember. I told him if he persisted I would have some people break both his legs."

Jesus's eyebrows rose high on his brow. "You did that?"

Alvaro laughed. "Of course not. How could the future deputy president of Spain do such a thing. I got somebody else to do it for me."

They both laughed. But the laughter soon died and Jesus's eyes were drawn to the vast edifice of the headquarters of the air force: the Army of the Air, they called it. They slipped past and onto the circus around the Arco de la Victoria of the Moncloa, brightly lit in the night. Sanchez pointed at it.

"Built by Franco to commemorate his victory against the Republicans. That civil war lasted three years, Alvaro, and was triggered by small, greedy men and women driven by ideology, who threatened murder and war, screaming across the floor at each other in Congress. Today reminded me of that. We cannot have that again."

Alvaro slapped him on the shoulder as the great stone arch swept by.

"Come on, Jesus! They were other times. The whole of Europe was destabilized, Germany's power was growing, Italy was torn between fascists and communists, the Balkans were unstable and everybody was terrified of what Russia might do next—"

Sanchez interrupted, half laughing. "Is this supposed to calm me? Are you talking about 1936 or 2023?" He wagged a finger at his friend. "And don't forget a very important dynamic, Alvaro, which we have today which was missing in '36. The stability of the past seventy years has not been thanks to the monolith of the European Union, it has been due to the steady flow of abundant energy to drive our industrial, commercial and social machinery. That energy is coming to an end, and we still have no credible alternative to replace it. And suddenly we find that Andalusia holds reserves that could keep us going for another century. That kind of power, Alvaro, can drive a man like Putin, or a man like Benjamin, to do crazy things."

They had left the Arco de la Victoria behind them and were now speeding among leafy suburbs toward the Palacio de la Moncloa, the president's official residence in Madrid. Alvaro was nodding.

"You're right," he said simply as they approached the Plaza Cardenal Cisneros underpass. Alvaro looked out the window to his left as a large SUV with tinted windows drew alongside. The front passenger window opened and a man in a balaclava leaned out with a pump action shotgun. He fired twice and their driver's head exploded in a shower of blood, gore and glass.

Jesus swore and screamed out his friend's name. Next thing the SUV rammed the Audi and drove it against the wall of the tunnel, spitting a shower of sparks up the grimy wall until the car came to a halt. Alvaro kicked open the rear door, smashing it against the rear of the van. He was screaming like a maniac. Jesus saw him grappling with a gunman. It was a second only, then the gunman was beating him to the ground. A fraction of a second later another man in a balaclava leaned in holding an assault rifle. Jesus said, "No," and the man emptied the magazine into the president of the government.

There were thirty-six rounds in the magazine. There was very little left of the president.

There were three men. They were wearing latex gloves, overalls and balaclavas. While two of them stripped off their masks and overalls, the third pulled a Glock 17 and put two rounds into Alvaro where he lay beside the car. He then stripped off his overalls and his mask too. All three men were completely bald.

There was chaos in the tunnel. Several cars had collided behind them and most of the traffic was trying to reverse away from the shooting. An Audi A4 pulled up. The three men climbed in and accelerated away to lose themselves in the spaghetti junction at Manzanares, just one mile away.

It was almost half an hour before the police cars, Guardia Civil antiterrorist squad and scene of crime forensic teams were able to get to the scene and cordon it off. Before that a helicopter ambulance flew in and found a badly beaten, injured Alvaro Romero on the road, and what was left of Jesus Sanchez, the president, in the back of his limousine.

When it was reported on the news the nation went into shock.

At twelve midnight a special, emergency session of parliament was called, and as Alvaro Romero entered the chamber, with his right arm in a sling and his face swollen and disfigured, purple and blue from the beating he had received, there was a collective gasp from all sides of the chamber. A doctor and a nurse attended him, but he walked, steady and unwavering, to the dispatch box. He didn't falter.

"Today, Spain has lost a great leader, a man who was an idealist and a pragmatist, a creative visionary, and a sound administrator, a politician who was also an incorruptible human being. Spain has lost all this, but I have lost more."

His tortured face twisted, his bottom lip curled in and he made no effort to hide his sobs. "I have lost all that, and also a brother and a friend. But I stand before you, the nation, here today and I tell you that the injuries I carry on my body are nothing compared to the injuries I bear in my heart and my soul! I am here to tell you that, as deputy president of the government I, here and now, step into the shoes of Jesus Sanchez, and if I stand here, talking to you, it is as though he were here himself!

"Whoever did this, I *swear* to you that they will not derail our dream and our project. I am ordering now, as of this very instant, the most thorough investigation into this brutal, savage murder. The investigation will be conducted by General Diego Carmona Sanchez, supreme commander of the Guardia Civil, and I swear to you on the blood of my fallen brother, that his death will be avenged and the enemies of Spain will be hunted down like rabid dogs and *exterminated!*"

There was heavy silence that spoke as much of shock as of awe before the extraordinary events that had risen before them. A moment later Alvaro Romero faltered and his doctor and his nurses rushed forward to support him. Seconds after that a gurney was rushed into the chamber and the acting president of the government was wheeled away.

The next day the press and the television news were completely dominated by, on the one hand the word "Exterminated," which appeared on just about every headline in Europe, and the question being asked by every congressman in Madrid, was the deputy president in a fit condition to step into the late president's shoes, or should they call a new general election. Benjamin Musa was among those vociferously calling for a general election. It would serve, he said, as a referendum to decide whether the people of Andalusia wanted to secede from Spain. But just about every right wing and moderate journalist and politician agreed that this was a time when Spain needed certainty and clarity, and a capable pair of hands. The dilemma was, was Alvaro Romero that pair of hands, or was he too emotionally and physically scarred to take charge of a powder keg as volatile as this one?

But, by that evening Alvaro Romero once again astonished the nation by appearing once again in public, this time on the steps of the Gregorio Marañon University Hospital, still with his arm in a sling and a badly battered face, but with a different demeanor and a different look in his eyes. He waved away the questions from reporters.

"I am going to make a simple statement. I am on my way now to the Moncloa to start work where Jesus Sanchez, the president, left off. Our program and our project for this country will continue unchanged. I will be briefed tonight on the progress of the investigation into Jesus's murder, and if I find there are adequate grounds, and that this was an act of terrorism by those wishing to tear this country apart, then I will declare a state of emergency. That is all I have to say for today."

His security team crowded around him and he was bundled down to his waiting car, and driven away into the growing dusk.

Maybe, as his car's red tail lights receded into the gathering gloom, he was thinking that his veiled threat would be enough to make Benjamin Musa back off. Maybe. Or perhaps he knew better than that.

In fact Benjamin Musa, already back in his corner office in Seville, had been working feverishly all day, calling in favors, applying thumbscrews and offering powerful inducements and bribes. He knew that this was his one shot. He would probably never get another. So he had to hit the bull right in the eye.

By the time Alvaro Romero climbed, exhausted into the back of his Audi, and took off for the palace of the Moncloa, Benjamin Musa was stretching out his legs and sipping a large Macallan whisky. He had secured an extraordinary, plenary session of the Andalusian Parliament for nine AM the next morning. He would make his case for independence, put forward a secondary motion for a referendum on independence, put both motions to the vote, and he knew— he knew because he had tied up every god damned loose end —he knew the motion for independence would be carried by a landslide majority.

He smiled, and then laughed. What a mess, he told

himself. What an almighty mess he had created! He threw back his head and laughed out loud. What an almighty, holy mess!

FOUR

I LANDED AT THE AIRPORT IN MALAGA UNDER THE molten glare of the midday sun. The other Andalusian airports at Seville, Jerez, Granada and Alicante, were closed to all but military and official flights.

The plane was practically empty because Spain was now, since the Andalusian Parliament had voted by eighty percent to twenty to declare itself an independent republic, officially a dangerous destination. You were better off on the Gaza Strip or swimming with sharks in South Africa than sunbathing on the desolate, barbed-wire beaches of the Costa del Sol.

The Spanish government, in the person of Alvaro Romero, had threatened the use of force and there had been a lot of table pounding and saber rattling, but the Spanish Foreign Legion, and half the top brass of those regiments based in Andalusia had said they would back Benjamin Musa, and by the next morning they had set up border checkpoints and passport controls on all major and minor roads and at all ports of entry.

Romero had been about to roll out the tanks and march in, but the king had remained silent, advocating words not war, and Brussels, the UN and NATO had all whispered in his ear that if he went to war against his own people, they would not be able to help.

Now the enraged Alvaro Romero was rattling not so much his saber as the hilt, having had the blade removed by his closest allies. Spain was spiraling into an ever deeper crisis, while Benjamin Musa and his separatists told CNN the Republic of Andalusia was too busy building oil rigs to worry about Spain's crises. And though NATO and the EU were popping metaphorical flowers into their rifle barrels, somewhere in the background you could hear the growing growl of tanks. Russian tanks.

The EU had appointed a negotiator, Comhghall ó Súilleabháin, a man with an unreasonable number of letters in his name, which ended up being simply Cowal O'Sullivan.

Cowal O'Sullivan had his work cut out for him. Nero had held me back a couple of days in DC while he observed O'Sullivan's lack of progress. Both sides were intransigent, Romero declaring that Musa's vote had been illegal and demanding NATO's support in retaking Andalusia, and Musa declaring that Spain was threatening to invade an independent, sovereign nation. The real crunch came when Moscow declared at the United Nations that it recognized Andalusia as an independent republic. Then Nero packed me onto a plane and sent me to Malaga.

The unspoken fear was that if Andalusia was successful in her bid, Catalonia and the Basque Country would not be far behind in jumping from the sinking ship. If that happened Spain would lose her industrial base. It was an open question whether the EU would allow that to happen, but what was worrying Nero was the possibility that the United States would end up being dragged into a global war the likes of which had not been seen for almost a hundred years. America's Ukraine on steroids.

Just a few weeks earlier the plane would have docked at one of the docking ports and a hundred or so passengers in straw hats and cargo shorts would have spilled out through the tunnels and into arrivals. But I guess the new Republic of Andalusia was on an economy drive until they started extracting their newer new oil, because the plane stopped on the tarmac and the twelve passengers who were on the plane had to climb down the steps and walk to customs and passport control across the melting tarmac.

I put on my heavy black sunglasses and squinted through the glare as I walked. It was kind of surreal to see the tanks and armored vehicles dotted around the runways, the machine gun emplacements and a couple of trucks with what looked like *Patriot* SAM trailers. It was a setup I had seen a hundred times before, but I had seen it in the Middle East and in Africa. I had never seen it in Europe.

Inside the terminal was vast, echoing and practically empty. Here and there, grunts stood around in twos and fours, with automatic weapons over their shoulders, smoking and looking worried, as though instead of eleven journalists and a representative from an oil consortium, the Spanish Army might descend from the plane, like the Achaeans from the Trojan Horse.

At the checkpoints the *Guardia Civil* stood with submachine guns, chewing gum and trying to look mean.

At passport control a guy in a green uniform eyed me and asked why I was visiting Andalusia. I told him I was interested in investing in Andalusian Oil, I had an appointment with Don Manuel Torreras Carbonell, the minister for oil, and papers granted by that ministry to travel freely within Andalusian borders. He scowled back at my passport, like he might find proof I was lying in there. Obviously he didn't, because he handed it back with a stamp saying I could stay for a month. I was pretty sure I wouldn't need that long.

I collected my Ford Mustang rental from the Hertz office in the lower levels of the parking lot and headed in toward the city. I was booked into the King Suite at the Marriott Malaga Palace, between the port at the cathedral. The port area of Malaga City is an attractive place. It has a long boulevard with exotic gardens and it's flanked on the south by the Mediterranean and on the north side by a long strip of elegant, 19th-century buildings overlooked by the Alkazaba, the medieval Arab citadel up the hills.

Whenever I had been there in the past it had been a bustling, lively place, with full restaurants and cafés, and large yachts and cruise ships moored in the port. Now it was practically deserted. There were few cars on the roads, most of the boats and ships in the harbor were gunmetal gray and bristling with guns and radar.

I pulled up outside the entrance, threw my keys to the valet and checked in at the front desk. The pretty blonde at the reception desk looked and sounded Russian. She smiled at me like I'd earned it by being rich, and snarled at the bellboy to take my case up to the room.

"Mr. Mason," she said, with more Rs than were strictly

necessary. "Ve heff message for you. It is delivered this morning."

She handed it over and I followed the bellboy, who had probably been on nodding terms with Methuselah, up in the elevator to the suite. He just about managed to open the curtains to the balcony and show me the bathroom and the bedroom before stopping for breath. I gave him twenty bucks and he walked carefully from the room, probably to die in the Ancient Bellboys' Graveyard, in the Land of Nod.

Once he'd gone I loosened my tie and opened the message.

Dear Mr. Mason,

Welcome to Malaga. Our mutual firend, Mr. Washington, has asked me to introduce you to Mr. Manuel Torreras Carbonel, at the Ministry of Oil. I will be glad to meet you for lunch this afternoon at the Refectorium Catedral. It is a short walk from your hotel, and I will be very happy to collect you at thirteen hundred hours and show you the way.

Mr. Torreras Carbonell has asked me to invite you to visit him tomorrow, if that is convenient. But we can discuss this over lunch. Please call me to confirm...

After that there was a telephone number and a signature above the printed name, A García.

"OUR MUTUAL FRIEND" was the term Nero had told me to look out for, and the misspelling of friend (firend) was confirmation that A Garcia was my contact within the Andalusian government. I had the number Nero had given me and I called it. It rang twice and went to an automatic answering service.

"This is a message for Mr. A Garcia from Alex Mason. Thank you for your message. I'll expect you at one PM and look forward to lunch at the Refectory."

I stepped into the shower, washed my hair and had a shave, and at twelve thirty I was dressing to go down and meet Garcia in the bar. As I splashed on my aftershave there was a tap at the door. I stepped out of the bathroom and opened up and saw a woman looking at me with large eyes that were closer to black than brown. Raymond Chandler would have described her as the kind of woman who'd make a bishop kick a hole in a stained glass window. For my part I was glad I wasn't a bishop.

She had smooth, pale skin, high cheekbones and a cupid's bow mouth that was trying not to smile. Her body was encased in a red satin dress that looked very happy to be where it was.

"Hola," I said, in very bad Spanish. The smile broke through with a touch of mocking.

"You are Alex Mason?"

"Probably."

"I think we have a mutual friend."

"Seriously? Remind me how you spell friend."

"You put the I before the R, like fire and end."

I frowned. "I was expecting Garcia. What happened."

Her eyes looked me over with a touch of insolence. "Nothing happened, Mr. Mason. I am Ana Garcia. Were you expecting an Antonio or an Alfredo? Are you disappointed?"

"*Disappointed* is not exactly the word. You're a little early." I said it as I went in to grab my jacket. She waited for me to come back and gave me the once-over again.

"Count yourself lucky. Most people in Andalusia are pathologically late. I thought we could have a chat and a drink before eating."

We stepped out into the midday sunshine of the Calle Larios, the pedestrianized street that runs through the center of the port area of the city. As we walked she linked her arm through mine and smiled up at me. I smiled back.

"Anything I should know before I meet Torreras tomorrow?"

"Oh, yes, plenty."

She didn't elaborate. I raised an eyebrow. "Care to elaborate?"

She laughed like I'd said something really funny. "No," she said and leaned her head on my shoulder. "What's that expression in English? It comes from archery." She made a gesture like she was pulling a bow. "Keeping tabs on somebody? I think that's what's happening right now. So for now we are just on a date. Do you think maybe you will enjoy a date with me?"

We rounded a corner. The cathedral rose, vast and imposing against the clear sky on our right. Directly opposite there was an elegant-looking restaurant with tables outside, set with brilliant white linen tablecloths, sparkling glasses and silver. She pointed.

"I think we should sit conspicuously, as though we have nothing to hide."

Her teeth were very white behind her very pink lips.

"Have we anything to hide?"

"Not yet, but anything can happen."

I held her chair while she sat, and took the seat opposite.

The waiter came and gave us menus. I ordered a couple

of martinis and while I studied the menu I asked her, "Who?" Then I frowned at the menu. "I mean, I am expected, right?"

She nodded. "The gambas pil-pil are very good if you like hot and spicy." I glanced up at her. She didn't meet my eye. "Americans are not the most popular people in the world here right now. So, yes, you are expected. But not many people believe you are who you say you are. So I am here to entertain you, try to draw out your real reason for being here, and meantime I am being watched."

She said all this to the menu while I let my eyes rove over her body, trying to visualize her with no clothes on and wondering if she had a wire. Modern wires were easy to hide. I wondered how sophisticated this tiny, embryonic republic's electronics might be. I decided the question was a fairly innocent one in the circumstances and asked, "Are you wearing a wire or a bug?"

"If I were, do you think I would tell you?"

I nodded. "Yes, because there is a pretty easy way to find out."

Her face contracted with sudden irritation. "This is not an intelligent conversation, after what I have told you. If we are being listened to—"

"If we are being listened to, then whoever is listening will hear the smart questions an American businessman is going to ask in the circumstances. There is not an investor in the USA who does not know that Russia, Saudi and Iran are all sniffing around Spain's skirts right now. So if I am going to invest my syndicate's money in Spanish oil, as I hope to, then I want to know how far Russia's influence goes, likewise with Iran and Saudi. If you are wearing a wire and we are being watched, then that is something I, and the people I represent, would want to know." I gave her a pleasant smile. "You're very attractive, Ana, but not enough to turn me into an idiot."

The smile I got in return was brittle with frost. "I am not wearing a wire." She dropped her menu on her plate and looked me directly in the eye. "And not just because our mutual friend has a very long reach and would punish me severely, but because I truly believe if Spain and Andalusia continue on this course we are going run into very serious problems. There could be war and hunger and economic chaos."

"That's fantastic, Ana." I laughed like I'd told a joke. She made a real effort and laughed too. Anyone watching would think I was flirting and coming on too strong, and she was being polite. I went on, "In any case, before you go I am going to have to have a look. You'll have to grin and bear it. Imagine I'm your gay friend. Our mutual friend is going to want to know you were clean."

She raised her hand and called the waiter. She ordered gambas pil-pil for two, a thing she called Iberian Secret for me and grilled salmon for herself.

"To drink we will have the Blanc Pescador which is light and sparkling and fruity, unlike me, and a Marques de Riscal for the meat and the salmon."

I smiled and for the first time meant it. "You're not light and sparkling and fruity, Ana?"

She shook her head and held my eye. "I am afraid that, unless I am working and putting on an act, I am a rather serious, boring girl. I don't go out, I don't party and I have only slept with one man in my life. He was my husband."

"Was?"

"He died. He was murdered."

"I am sorry. I didn't mean to pry."

"It is OK. I invited the conversation, because I want you to know I am not flirting with you." She leaned forward and laughed. "I am putting on an act for our audience. So far, Mr. Mason, I don't like you very much."

I raised my glass. "The feeling is entirely mutual." We laughed and toasted.

FIVE

WE TALKED ABOUT THE QUALITY OF LIFE IN
Andalusia since the declaration of independence. We
talked about countries she had visited and how good her
English was, and then we talked about stereotypes of
Spanish food and American food. She took a moment to
explain to me that everyone from Pernambuco and
Tierra del Fuego to Alaska was an American, and I
thanked her for that insight. After that we made plans
for the next day and she told me she would collect me at
nine thirty AM to take me to meet Mr. Torreras
Carbonell.

Then we went back to my hotel where I made her strip.
She had no wire and no bug, but I already knew that because
the cell phone ODIN had provided me with alerted me if
there was a transmitting device within ten feet, but she had
got on my nerves so I decided to make her jump through a
hoop or two.

As she was stepping out of the door I told her, "Say,

Ana, make it ten, will you? At nine I have to make a couple of phone calls."

She stood staring at me a moment before nodding.

"Of course, Mr. Mason. I will inform the minister."

"Thanks, Ana, you're a doll. You have a great evening. I'll see you tomorrow."

The door closed a little more forcefully than was perhaps necessary and I dropped onto the sofa in the drawing room, twiddling my thumbs and wondering if anything important had just happened. I had just decided there was no way of knowing when my cell rang.

"Hey Boss—"

"You have decided to add vulgarity to facetiousness to complete your repertory of obnoxious habits."

"Ana Garcia would probably agree with you."

"Your contact."

"How sure of her are you?"

"As sure as we can ever be, which is not very sure, but she is the only contact we have. So try not to antagonize her. Though from what you say that ship has already sailed."

"I made her strip so I could check for a wire."

"Your cell provides for that eventuality. As I say, vulgar and facetious. You are meeting Torreras tomorrow."

"Yes," I said, without indulging in facetiousness or vulgarity.

"Good, we hope he will give you guidelines regarding investment. By the way, did you tell your wife you were going to Malaga?"

I paused half a beat while I took onboard what he was telling me. "No. She gets jealous when I go abroad. Has she said something to you?"

"No, but Sally heard her on the phone the other day and she was telling her friends she thought you were in Spain."

"One of these days I'm going to have to do something to shut her up. Have a word with her and get back to me, will you?"

"I'll see what I can do."

He hung up and I sat thinking. It wasn't sophisticated, but it was the best he could do at short notice. Somebody was breaching our security and eavesdropping on our electronic communications. The Russians and the Chinese had huge resources and capabilities in electronic eavesdropping, and every day it was getting harder for the Five Eyes to keep ahead of them. But what troubled me most was the fact that the cutting-edge encryption software the Five Eyes were currently using was so deep and so complex it had been rated virtually impossible to decode, unless you had some kind of key. That had been the unanimous opinion of a group of the leading IT experts available to the Pentagon.

That meant that either Russia had been given decoding software by the aliens they had imprisoned at Kapustin Yar, or they had a mole inside ODIN who had given them a key. Call me a skeptic, but I was inclined to go with the latter explanation. That meant electronic communication with Nero had to be kept to an absolute minimum until further notice, and what little communication there was would have to be creative, to say the least.

I spent the day visiting the Picasso museum and showing myself around the Alcazaba, the port and the lighthouse. While I was out and about I bought myself half a dozen burners at different stores around town. Then I went and had a look at the lighthouse. It had, apparently, been there since before the Phoenicians, and the most recent research suggested it was older even than that, going back to the times of the mythical city of Tartessos, inhabited by proto-Celtic peoples who spoke an early form of Celtic which dated back to the Tower of Babel.

It all stirred up old interests of mine I had neglected for years; in fact, since I had first met Nero on Victoria Island, in the Bay of Bengal. Archeology, he had told me back then, was the very venerable practice of investigating people's activities in circumstances where they were virtually undiscoverable. And once discovered, he added, they had virtually no impact on life, the universe or anything. Counterespionage on the other hand, he said, was pretty much the same thing, but the outcome could have a profound effect on life, the universe and everything.

I stood on the long pier in the late-afternoon sunshine, with the Mediterranean wind battering me, and thought about a pet theory of mine: that Homer's Mycenae had in fact been the legendary city of Tartessos, a powerhouse of metallurgy and mining which depended almost entirely on the Cornish tin mines for the manufacturing of bronze. A power struggle had arisen between the kingdom of Troy, in southern England (Truro?), and Tartessos, in southern Spain, that had erupted into a war that had overturned the balance of power and changed the course of history for the next five or six thousand years or more.

The theory reduced Helen to no more than a metaphor for bronze, or, worse, tin, which meant it was a theory most classicists, historians and archeologists would laugh at. But right then, as I stood looking out at the flat, sparkling Med, I didn't care much about what the so-called experts thought. I was thinking about how fragile the balance of world power was, how easy it was for those in power to upset it if they put their minds to it, and above all, how little they cared about the thousands—in some cases millions—of lives that were sacrificed in their obsessive pursuit of that power.

In the mists of prehistory, as we emerged from the late Stone Age into the Bronze Age, the source of wealth and power was tin. Now, as we emerged from the post-industrial era into whatever awaited us in the new millennium, it was oil. But the name of the game was the same: to seize and control that source of power.

Tartessos re-emergent.

I made my way back along the seafront, through the Parque de Malaga to the hotel. I showered and changed, thought about inviting Ana for dinner, but decided against it and dined alone with a book before having an early night.

AT NINE FIFTY the next morning reception buzzed me that Ms. Garcia was waiting for me. I stood on the balcony looking at the sea until ten and then went down to meet her. She was dressed in a severe dark blue pants suit, sitting in a large leather chair and looked at her watch as I stepped out of the elevator. She stood as I approached and kissed me on both cheeks. I didn't take it personally. It's what they do in Spain.

She led me outside, where there was a dark blue Audi waiting, with a uniformed chauffeur standing by the rear door. He opened it and Ana slipped in gracefully, and I walked around to the far door and got in under my own steam.

The drive was all of five hundred yards, out of the hotel, down the Paseo del Parque, and left to the building the Junta had requisitioned from the University of Malaga and handed over to the brand-new Ministry for Petroleum Research, or *Ministerio de la Investigación Petrolífera.*

Two armed guards stood either side of the entrance and checked Ana's ID before we went inside. We crossed an oxblood and cream checkerboard marble floor, and what looked like a genuine nineteenth-century concertina elevator took us up to the fourth floor. There we followed a passage to the back of the building where a woman with hair like concrete and a face like distilled bile sat behind a large, wooden desk and picked up a telephone. She muttered something quiet and private into the receiver and pointed at the door. It buzzed and we went through.

Mr. Manuel Torreras Carbonell, the Minister for Oil, was spherical and shiny. His bald head was shiny, his round, hairless face was shiny and his round, wire-framed spectacles were shiny. You got the impression when you looked at him that he didn't wash in the morning so much as polish himself.

He stood as we walked in, grinned and spread his arms wide.

"Mr. Mason, Mr. Mason, Mr. Mason! It is a great pleasure for me to greet you and welcome you to our young republic at such an exciting time for us."

He advanced on me, grabbed me by the upper arms and proceeded to lean on my right shoulder and then on my left. I figured that was what guys did instead of kissing. Then he clapped both shoulders and said, "*Magnifico, magnifico!*" Then, gesturing to a chair at his desk that looked like a minor throne, "Please, sit, will you have coffee? Tea?"

I heard the door close behind me. Ana had left.

"Thank you," I said, glancing at the door, "I have just had breakfast."

We sat and he smiled a big, happy, shiny smile. "Now, Mr. Mason, how can the Republic of Andalusia help you?"

"Well," I sat back and crossed one leg over another, "I represent a consortium of American investors who would be very interested in investing in your oil, and perhaps in helping you to build the infrastructure you need to extract and exploit that oil."

He stared at me for an unnerving length of time, with his shiny smile fixed to his face. It was like he'd left the smile there while he went away to think. Finally he blinked.

"Of course, but there are things we do not really understand."

"Oh?"

He hunched his shoulder, spread his hands. "Your government is not recognizing us. This is hurtful for a young country like ours. It makes it difficult and embarrassing for us."

"It is very early days, Mr. Torreras. You only made your declaration of independence a week ago."

"This is true." He still had his shoulders hunched. "But we must think, ask ourselves, if your government does not recognize us, will they allow you to invest? Will there be sanctions, barriers...?"

I nodded in a way I hoped conveyed sageness and worldly experience. "I understand your misgivings, Mr. Torreras. However, I assure you that our investors can operate through offshore companies that would not be subject to US Government controls."

He simpered. "Of course we are very fortunate to have a few friends in the world. The Russians have been very helpful and they also are offering us assistance with building up our infrastructure. Iran, who are very knowledgeable in the field of oil drilling and exploitation..." He trailed off, then looked as if he had shocked himself. "Oh! Please! I do not mean that we are not interested in your offer! We are always delighted to cultivate good friendships. What I mean to say is that, at this early stage, the friendships of governments are very important to us. So, more than money or technical help, your assistance in promoting a positive relationship with your government would be most helpful."

I frowned and stroked my chin. "I see. Well, that is not beyond the bounds of possibility, Mr. Torreras, but neither is it easy. As you know, the United States and Russia have a difficult relationship at the moment. Before I can intercede on your behalf, I would need to know a little bit about the extent to which Andalusia is friends with Russia."

He gave a squeaky, wheezing laugh. "I understand! Believe me I understand! What can I tell you? Our Russian friends have taken an interest in our development and our progress. The Iranians and other oil-producing countries have also viewed us sympathetically."

I looked at the window that overlooked the port and the avenue where palm trees and plane trees swayed silently in the sea breeze.

"Let me see," I said, "if I understand you. You might look favorably on our investments if we were willing to lobby Congress to recognize your independence from Spain as a separate nation." He started to answer but I cut him short. "However, you are not willing to confide in me the extent to which Russia and Iran are helping you."

"Mr. Mason, you put it like that and it sounds very unreasonable, but you must understand that we must be very careful. Though I am certain you are a very honorable and upright man, the truth is we do not know you, and you might be an agent working for the US Government to undermine our relationship with the Kremlin, and our bid for independence."

I crossed my arms and thrust out my lower lip while I made a show of thinking. "What," I said finally, "would I have to do to gain your trust?" He went to answer but I held up a hand. "Don't rush your answer, Mr. Torreras. I don't want you to dismiss possibilities just because you think they might be unrealistic. We wield a lot of power as a consortium, and we have seen the future without oil. Believe me, it does not look bright. So we are willing to go the extra mile to make this work. Think about it—what would we have to do to gain your trust in a full, deep and far-reaching negotiation? What we would need would be a fuller understanding of your relationship with Russia and Iran. What would *you* need in order to give us that understanding?"

His face was the picture of a shiny, happy apple. "Thank you, Mr. Mason, for being so open and honest. A good start would be an assurance that you do not, umm, work, shall we say, for the US Government."

"I can give you that assurance right now."

"Yes, of course, and I would not dream of doubting your word. However, some kind of proofs, some kind of evidences..."

I frowned. "What kind of evidence?"

He spread his hands again. "Maybe some proof of your consortium, documents, the CEO, some proof of this nature that you are who you say you are, and that you can make pressure on your government."

I nodded. I wasn't crazy about the turn the conversation was taking. I sighed. "Let me talk to Austin—"

He frowned. "Austin?"

"Texas, and see what they can come up with. Meantime, some show of good will on your part would go a long way toward helping."

He nodded several times with his eyes closed. "Of course, Mr. Mason. Let me talk also with Mr. Romero, our president, and see what he would find satisfactory. Meanwhile, would you accept an invitation to view our oil fields in Granada? I am sure you will find them very interesting. We are working very hard there to establish the first rigs to begin extraction. *Señorita* Garcia would be very happy to show you. She is satisfactory. You would like somebody else?"

I gave him a meaningful smile. "*Señorita* Ana is very satisfactory."

"Good! Excellent! Shall we meet again, then, Mr. Mason, say the day after tomorrow, and see what our bosses have to say?"

"That sounds fine."

He pressed a button on his desk, rattled something in Spanish that included, *Señorita* Garcia, and stood, extending his hand to me across the desk. I was dismissed. I stood and took his hand.

"One thing the consortium members were concerned

about, Mr. Torreras, was the assassination of Jesus Sanchez. Are you investigating that?"

He offered me a bland, shiny smile. "That was a murder which occurred in Spain, Mr. Mason, beyond our jurisdiction. Alas, we are unable to investigate it. But I can assure you, it had absolutely nothing to do with us."

I squeezed his hand and smiled. "That is a great comfort, Mr. Torreras."

Behind me the door opened. Ana Garcia was waiting for me.

SIX

TORRERAS HAD HAD A BRIEF DISCUSSION WITH ANA while I waited in his secretary's antechamber. After five minutes Ana had emerged from his office and led me down in the concertina elevator and out through the lobby to the midmorning sun.

"You want to walk," she said. It wasn't a question.

I pointed across the road to the Malaga Park that bordered the avenue. "Let's take a stroll. Allow me to buy you lunch on the port."

As we crossed the road I checked my cell to see if she was wearing a wire. She wasn't.

We crossed at the lights and headed east along the broad sidewalk with the trees on our right. The harsh caw of the parakeets, and the sudden explosions of flapping as a dozen or more burst from the trees, made the place seem more tropical than Mediterranean.

She took my arm and I said, "Tell me about Jesus Sanchez."

She didn't look at me. She stuck out her lower lip and gave her head a single shake.

"I wish I could."

"What does that mean, Ana?"

"It means I know what you know." She glanced up at me. Her hair, pulled back in a low bun, looked very black, with brilliant reflections from the sun. Her eyes were a deep brown. "He was assassinated by professionals who knew where he was going to be at that time on that day." She was quiet for a moment, looking at the trees while we walked. "I have made discreet inquiries, I have engaged members of the intelligence and security communities in," she shrugged and gave me an ironic look, "*innocent* conversations about it. Nobody knows anything. I have overheard Musa discussing it with his security advisors, and I would put my hand on the Bible and swear he did not know who killed Sanchez."

We turned in among the trees, following the winding, unpaved paths, littered with leaves, stones and moss.

"Does that worry you?" I asked her.

Her answer was immediate. "Yes, it does. Because if Sanchez had lived, there would have been a protracted period of debate in parliament, in Brussels, in the United Nations, and whatever conclusion was arrived at would have the solid foundations of international debates and agreements. And at the end of that period there would almost certainly have been a referendum." She looked up at me again. "These are the things that give a nation roots and stability."

"But that didn't happen."

She nodded. "That didn't happen. He was assassinated in his car with his oldest, closest friend and ally beside him.

They should both have died, but Romero survived, and emerged from the crisis bitter, angry and full of hatred for Musa and for the whole of Andalusia, swearing vengeance on the south."

"That precipitated a premature declaration of independence—"

"And, because the Basque Country and Catalonia are thinking about following, it forces Spain into either declaring war on Andalusia, to hold the kingdom together, or disintegrating and vanishing as a nation, like Yugoslavia. War is all but guaranteed."

"War is all but guaranteed," I echoed. "So who would benefit from a civil war in Spain?"

She hunched her shoulders and screwed up her face. It should have been an ugly expression, but on her it managed to look beautiful.

"*Nobody.*" It was a helpless statement of bewilderment.

"Well, let's take it slowly, one step at a time." I slowed my pace as we moved through the dappled shade. "Another way of putting down deep roots and cultivating national unity, is to fight a common enemy and win. Musa might have gambled that if Andalusia left the kingdom of Spain, taking tourism, agriculture and oil with her, Catalonia and the Basques might be tempted to do the same, believing they might prosper more in Europe as independent states. Which, from what you say, is what is happening. That way, Spain's military power crumbles without having fired a single shot."

She thought about it, leaning against me slightly as we walked. Eventually she said, "No." I waited. She said, "No, because Musa had already secretly negotiated the support of

Russia and Iran, and the risk of a severe retaliation from Spain, supported by NATO was too great," she waved her left hand in the air, "whether in open conflict or by using paramilitary, special forces or organizations like your CIA. The risk of foreign intervention was too great."

"OK—"

"Besides, as I told you, I have heard him in conversation with his security advisors, and he does not know who killed Sanchez. It has caused him problems. He would have preferred a protracted battle with Jesus."

There was some sense in what she said. I knew the answer to my own question, but I asked her anyway. "So, if not Musa, who?"

She shrugged and looked helpless again. "Someone who would have an interest in..."

She trailed off. I said, "In fostering a civil war in Spain."

"Who could possibly have an interest in that?"

We had come to some steps that descended to the narrow, shaded road that separates the port from the park. She trotted down ahead of me and turned to watch me descend. I stood in front of her and looked long and hard into her eyes, trying to read what was there. All I could find was a sincere, sensitive woman who had been used by life as a football for a few years.

"There is one, very obvious candidate, Ana. I am going to tell you, and then I want you to think very hard about the years and months leading up to Sanchez's assassination, to see if anything leaps out at you to confirm that theory. I also want you to be very alert to what happens in the next few days, for the same reason."

She screwed up her face. "Who?"

"The Russians."

She rolled her eyes and turned away from me. "You Americans, always obsessed with the Russians, reds under the bed. Paranoia."

She crossed the road and started climbing the broad, white marble steps to the port. I went after her, took her arm as she reached the top of the steps and turned her to face me.

"You have just been an active participant in a *coup d'état* against the Spanish state, and while you were at it you were conspiring with the United States Government to provide them information to help reverse the coup. I don't think you're in any position to be calling people paranoid." She drew breath, I cut her short. "Don't tell me, it's different."

She used the breath she'd drawn to sigh. She turned away and started walking slowly toward the restaurants and cafés that lined the harbor a couple of hundred yards away. I kept pace with her.

"Did you know that the CIA virtually engineered the war in Afghanistan?"

She glanced at me. "It wouldn't surprise me."

"Do you think the Russian FSB is all about compassion and loving kindness?"

"I am not that naïve."

"I hope not, because I am going to need your help; and if, as I suspect, the Russians were behind Sanchez's murder, we have one big problem on our hands and the last thing I need is you going naïve on me."

"I told you, I am not."

"Believe me, it would be very much in the Russians' interest to spark a civil war within the European Union, especially if it drew NATO into the conflict."

She gave me that look certain Europeans reserve for certain non-Europeans that's all about being ancient and having lots of very old universities and tracing their origins back to Ancient Greece.

"How can NATO intervene in a Spanish civil war? NATO will intervene if a non-NATO nation attacks a NATO ally. Not if a NATO ally attacks itself."

I gave her that look I reserve for cocky young women I want to put across my knee and spank until their cheeks turn pink. We had reached the restaurants and she had stopped at a table where a waiter in a white jacket pulled out a chair for her and she sat, watching me with very little expression. I sat and told the waiter to bring two martinis, dry.

"Oh," I said and smiled. "I didn't know that. Can you explain something to me then? What would happen if a NATO country like Spain was sliding toward civil war and a foreign country was shown to be intervening by supplying one side with weapons and soldiers?"

She suppressed a small, patronizing sigh. "There is no way Russia would put itself in that situation. And isn't that exactly what the USA and Europe have been doing in Ukraine?"

"Of course she wouldn't. But she might well provide Iran with intelligence, real or false, suggesting that in exchange for military help Musa and the Andalusian government might look favorably on a considerably expanded Iranian presence here. And if the Islamic population became large enough..." I left the words hanging. "Do you think NATO would shrug and turn a blind eye to that? Because if you do, you're more naïve than I thought."

Her cheeks colored pink and that gave me a certain amount of unedifying satisfaction.

"I imagine," she said, with her eyes bright and her lips tight, "that in those circumstances NATO, and particularly the USA, would want to take some pretty urgent action. But whatever you may think about the ayatollahs, I don't think the Iranian government is that stupid."

"They don't need to be patient. They just need to be ill informed. I don't know why you are kicking against me so much today, but all I am asking you to do is to think back over the last year and examine the contact the Russians had with Musa's wider team. In retrospect, was there any indication they might have been planning to assassinate Sanchez? And, in the light of what is going down now, is there any chance Iran's decision to help Andalusia is a prelude to a much heavier intervention, backed by Russia?"

She gazed out at the ships moored behind me. "Yes," she said, and shrugged. "Of course it's possible."

"Then that said, why is it so difficult for you to think back and see if there are any particular incidents, meeting or simple facts that spring to mind that might support that possibility?" She didn't answer and I went on. "I have to say, Ana, for a woman who came to us asking for help, you have a very odd attitude. I can't help wondering what the hell is going on. Am I going to get the knock on the door tonight at four AM?"

"Of course not."

"There is no 'of course' about it, Ana. The mortality rate in this job is high."

"Is that a threat?"

I never threaten women, children or small fluffy animals. So what's going on?"

The motion was sudden. She jerked forward and put her elbows on the table and buried her face in her hands.

"I have been told to seduce you and get pillow talk from you!"

I watched her and laughed, and spoke at the same time. "On my count of three you are going to flop back in you chair and we are both going to laugh out loud like you were telling a funny story. Or you will be dead by tonight."

I leaned back in my chair and roared. After a second she did the same thing, and the waiter arrived with our drinks and a couple of menus. As he retreated I raised my glass to her and we toasted and drank. Still chuckling I set down my glass and leaned forward, like I was coming on to her.

"I will not sleep with you, Ana. So you can chill on that score. But even if I did, you wouldn't get any pillow talk out of me. You spend a couple of nights in my suite and we'll feed them information."

She put her hand on mine and smiled. I had no idea whether she was acting or genuine. "Thank you, but I can't shake the feeling I am betraying my country."

"Well, you have to make a decision. Is your country Andalusia, or Spain?"

She took my hand in both of hers now and stroked it with her thumbs. I hoped to Christ she was acting. She said, "OK, thank you. You are not so bad after all, I guess."

"I can think of a few people who might disagree. But thanks anyhow. I'll tell you what I want right now. A hamburger with fries."

She laughed, called the waiter and told him we wanted two burgers and two cold beers. Then she became serious.

"This afternoon I am to take you to Baza, in Granada. We will stay at the Hotel Anabel. It was two stars. We have adjoining rooms. We will visit the oil fields, where they are drilling, and then, tonight, I must seduce you."

I picked up my martini and frowned at the olive. "Be gentle," I said. "I'm still a virgin."

For a moment her face contracted with anger, but then she laughed.

SEVEN

THE MINISTRY WANTED ME TO USE THEIR AUDI and their driver. I told them I had an aversion to Audis because bad guys always drove either Audis or BMWs. They had absolutely no idea what I was talking about, but they didn't argue either. So in the end we took my Mustang. I told Ana that good guys always drove either Mustangs or classic Jaguars, but she had no idea what I was talking about either.

It was a two and a half hour drive from Malaga to Baza, through some of the weirdest landscapes I had seen in a long time. Once past Granada, as you start to climb into the mountains, much of the terrain starts to turn red, huge red rock formations jut suddenly out of gray deserts and, as you look closely at them, you see that the rocks have doors and windows cut into them. Because in this part of Spain people still live in caves.

Past Guadix, up in the Sierra Nevada, things got remote. There are plenty of places in the States which get remote.

Alaska is about as remote as you can get while staying on the planet. Even New Mexico, Arizona and Nevada can be pretty remote. But it's a different kind of remoteness. There you are remote in space. This was more like being remote in time.

We drove past places with names like Gor, Baúl and Bacor, and a megalithic park where dolmens and megaliths stood solitary, in the middle of a field, dating back to long before man had learned how to make metal. There were no people and the roads were practically empty of cars. Ana must have noticed my expression because she suddenly laughed and said, "This is what we call *la España profunda*. It means the deep Spain. It is very dark, very Catholic, very repressed. There is still a lot of ignorance here, and the parish priest and the sergeant of the Guardia Civil are the law still."

I was going to make a crack about it sounding like New England, but that wouldn't have been fair to New England, and she wouldn't have known what the hell I was talking about again.

Pretty soon after Gor and the standing stones, the earth started to turn a pale, ash-gray, the olive trees became stunted and twisted and the temperature began to rise. You got the feeling this wasn't a desert because the people didn't allow it to be, but whatever the earth gave, it gave grudgingly.

Ana said suddenly, "Baza, Bacor, especially Baúl, people like to pretend they are Arab names, but they are much older. The names that begin with Ba, they honor the Mesopotamian god Baal. This is a very ancient place."

I nodded. I believed her. I could feel it.

Shortly after that we entered the town and came to the hotel Anabel. This was a two-star hotel, so there was no valet parking and no buttons. We made our way up to the third floor in an elevator that had been all the rage in the 1970s, dumped our cases in our rooms, which were basic and clean, and headed straight out again for the oil fields. It was closing on noon.

The fields were some six or seven miles from the town of Baza, headed north along the A-4200. The road was straight and all around the terrain was flat and in varying shades of gray and rust. It was a desolate landscape in which even the sparse olive trees looked ancient, skinny and thirsty.

Eventually, about a mile short of the town of Benamaurel, Ana told me to turn right onto a dirt track which was covered in an almost luminous white powder. As we lurched and ground up the track, a huge plume of white dust rose into the hot air, trailing behind us like a host of talcum powder ghosts. We came to a narrow canal, crossed a small bridge and fifty yards on, down a dusty, white path we came to a twenty-foot steel fence, behind which, ten feet on, there was another twenty-foot steel fence, and in between the two fences were rolls of razor wire: more effective than dogs and less likely to eat drugged steaks.

There were steel doors in each fence, and at each door there were two soldiers with assault rifles. At a glance they looked like HK416s, but a closer glance told me they were Iranian Masaf 5.56s.

I glanced at Ana as the gate was rolled open. "Are you aware they are carrying Iranian rifles?"

"No, I didn't know that."

We followed the track across a flat, white desert dotted with small, gnarled bushes like small, green clenched fists. Above us the sky was white-blue and the temperature, according to the car, was a searing forty-eight centigrade: one hundred and twenty F.

Pretty soon we began to see the massive rigs being erected to start drilling, with guys in yellow hats and no shirts scrambling all over them. The site was massive. It must have been several miles square, and besides the rigs, we could also make out trucks, bulldozers and diggers laying the foundations for the roads and the buildings—the basic infrastructure—that would soon smother this desert landscape. Oil had come to town.

We followed the track down for half a mile and eventually came to a stack of cabins piled on top of each other with makeshift staircases connecting the different floors. There was another steel fence around these, though the gates hung open. I found a space between a couple of Land Rovers and Grenadier and parked. As we climbed out a couple of men emerged from the office two floors up and trotted down the stairs. One of them was in jeans and a T-shirt. The other was in a suit, with a reflective jacket over the top. He was balding and his black glasses made his tanned head look like a dark brown ball.

At the bottom of the stairs he muttered something to the guy in jeans, who gave me a look that was as friendly as a grizzly with a mad ferret up its ass, and walked away to climb into a Toyota truck. As he drove away, the bald guy approached Ana with both hands outstretched.

"Ana, Ana," he said, like once just wasn't enough. "Always a pleasure to see you. And who is this fortunate man who rides with you? He must be Mr. Mason. Mr. Mason, what a great pleasure and an honor to welcome you to our enterprise."

He let go of Ana's hand and clasped my right in both of his. Both of his were perspiring.

"How do you do?" I asked, injecting indifference into my smile. I used my now damp hand to indicate the gray desert around me. "You're not wasting time, are you?"

"Time!" he said, raising his eyebrows high on his shiny head. "There is too little of it to waste. Andalusia needs us to produce oil, quickly, quickly!"

Ana intervened. "Mr. Mason, this is Dr. Jose Carlos Montilla, the chief engineer in charge of overseeing the construction and development of the wells." She turned to Dr. Montilla. "Mr. Mason represents an American consortium—"

"Oh, I know all about Mr. Mason! I have had the minister for oil on the telephone telling me to take specially good care of you! And show you everything you would like to see, and give you every assistance possible. So, Mr. Mason, I am completely at your service."

"Good to know. Well, to begin with, why don't you go over the basics for me, and we'll see what questions emerge as we go along?"

He spread his arms wide and smiled, like all of life was just a fountain of delight for him. "As you wish!" he told me and went to one of his pre-fab offices and returned with three reflective jackets and three bright yellow safety hats. He gestured at a Toyota truck. "Let's take my truck and I will show you around."

We pulled on the gear, I climbed into the front passenger seat and Ana got in the back and we pulled out of the enclosure into the wider desert. The earth, for as far as you could see, was parched, white clay. We turned right out of the gate and then headed south into what looked like a vast, ancient river valley. I could make out a team working on a broad, asphalt road half a mile away on my right. Dr. Montilla jerked his head at them.

"They make the principal road that goes from the center of the field to the national road where you have come. From the center more roads will branch out, like a star, to each of the wells. Also we will extend to here a railway line, and there will be, of course, pipelines from here to Malaga and Cadiz. Special ports will have to be built."

"How many wells have you started so far?"

"In this site twelve, with twelve more projected. I can send you the details of other sites in Almeria, Malaga and Cadiz. These are the principal ones."

"Has Andalusia the engineers to build pipelines to carry crude oil that far? And how about the refineries? Have you got experts to take care of that? I know we would love to supply you with that kind of expertise."

He laughed a big, happy laugh as we bounced over rocks and potholes toward a half-built rig a mile away.

"You are come too late, my friend Mason. We have Russian engineers who are already talking with Andalusian engineers at the universities of Seville, Jaen and Granada, drawing up the plans for the pipelines."

"What about experts on the ground to build them? We can supply—"

He was waving his hand in the air and laughing again. I guess he felt this was a moment of triumph for Spain over the USA, his moment of personal revenge for Manila Bay and Santiago de Cuba, and the destruction of the Spanish fleet.

"No, no, no, thank you. We do not need American help. We have Iranian experts who will come and work beside Spanish workers to build this pipeline." He offered me a radiant smile. "Nobody know more about oil pipelines than the Russians and the Iranians, I think!"

It was all a bit too easy and I wondered if I was being deliberately fed this information. I took it and assimilated it and added a touch of salt.

"So, in what way can we help you, Dr. Montilla? When I spoke to the minister this morning he seemed to think that, provided we could solve a couple of security issues, he would welcome American help."

He negotiated a small hill where we skidded slightly on the loose, chalk-like dust. As we straightened out he nodded vigorously. "Oh, of course, we are always welcome help. When you say America, I think you refer to the United States. America is very big, Mexico, Panama, Guatemala, Honduras, El Salvador, Colombia—"

"Yeah," I cut him short before he listed all the countries on the American continents. "They are all part of America," I said, "but the only one that has America in its name, is the United States of America. That's our name. So, I would be very happy to know, Dr. Montilla, in what way could the United States of America help Andalusia to get on its feet economically?"

He swung the steering wheel and we lurched off the road and started hurtling across the scrubland toward a massive structure that looked like something out of *Mad Max*.

"Well, Mr. Mason," he said, showing me a smile that was looking ever more strained. "You could begin by recognizing us as an independent nation!"

"I'd love to. Believe me, nothing would give me more pleasure, but that is for the politicians. What I can do is offer you concrete, practical assistance in the way of labor, expertise, materials and machinery to help turn that black gold into money in the bank."

He began to slow as we approached the massive structure. "At what price, Mr. Mason? Will we have to sell our new independence to the USA? Will the USA take possession of our oil? What is the price?"

I laughed. "Again, Dr. Montilla, neither you nor I can negotiate the price. That is for your political leaders and the heads of my consortium to sit down around the table and reach an agreement which is good for all sides. If it were up to me, Dr. Montilla, I'd give it to you for free. But that's not my job and it's not in my gift. All I can do is find out in what ways we can help you, and communicate it back to my bosses."

He glanced at me and drew breath. I cut him short before he could take another pot shot at the stereotype.

"I'd also ask you a question. You seem to have thrown in your lot with Russia and Iran. I don't know to what extent, but if you take a look at what they are asking in return for all this help, it might be worth your while seeing what the USA has to offer. Because I can guarantee you that the USA will do just about anything to stop Russia and Iran getting a foothold in Europe."

It was a gamble, but my gut told me that the good doctor would enjoy nothing more than letting me know how hopeless the American situation was, and how well entrenched the Russians and the Iranians were. And that was pretty much all I wanted to know.

We were just a couple of hundred yards away from a vast circular structure made of huge steel bars assembled into a kind of scaffolding. Inside the structure a giant drill was pounding at the earth, sending up vast plumes of dirty gray dust, high into the air. He slowed and took a very deep breath.

"Speaking only as an engineer, Mr. Mason, and nothing personal against you, right now I have everything I need from the Russians and the Iranians. In the future I cannot say. Maybe thing will change, and we need help from USA. But right now, all I can say is maybe the government will allow you to invest money in shares. But everything like machines, hardware, software, labor, expertise, all this we are getting from our friends in the East, at a price." He smiled and shook his head. "A price, Mr. Mason, you cannot compete with."

"Why's that?"

"Because it is free. They charge us nothing."

I nodded a few times. "Free?"

"Free."

"I don't need to convince you, Doctor, because neither you nor I am in a position to make decisions. But I will remind you that there is no such thing as a free lunch. You either pay now, or you pay later, but pay you will."

I trailed off as he drew to a halt, and my eyes picked out a broad expanse of dark, sage green several miles away. At first I thought they were odd, symmetrical areas of pinewoods, or olive groves, but as I peered through the dusty air and the shimmering heat I realized what they were. They were several acres of olive-green tents. I pointed.

"What's that?"

I watched his face. It tried to hide two or three reactions before he smiled and said, "Plant."

"Plant?"

"Mainly machinery, materials, this kind of thing. Nothing of interest."

I held his eye and gave him just the ghost of a smile; a polite one.

"It looks like a military camp."

After a moment he turned his head and looked at the orderly, oblong patches of military camouflage. Then he turned back to me and there was a trace of insolence in his smile. "Yes," he said, "I suppose it does." Then, looking past my shoulder his smile broadened. "Ah, Mr. Mason, here is somebody I wanted you to meet. I dispatched my assistant to go and find her when you arrived." He laughed his shiny laugh again. "It seems our independence has attracted all of Islam's enemies to our shores!"

Ana and I turned. The woman I saw approaching looked as good in jeans and a khaki shirt as she did in a violet satin evening dress with a slash all the way up her right leg. She was frowning at me with her eyebrows but smiling with her mouth. Dr. Montilla said, "Mr. Alex Mason, meet Captain Aila Gallin, of the Israeli Petroleum Research Institute."

EIGHT

Two thousand five hundred miles away, to the north and east, Colonel Alexandrina Vitsin exhaled smoke from her nose and mouth and stubbed out her cigarette in her ashtray. She rasped, "Come," and the door to her dark office opened.

Oleg Babanin, a man in a badly cut suit stepped inside and, with elaborate care, he turned, bent slightly at the waist, and closed the door behind him. Then he turned to the colonel and smiled, as though hoping she approved.

"Doors," he said, "doors and windows, always closed. No?"

Vitsin did not answer. A beam of sunlight leaned in through the window that overlooked Mokhovaya Ulitsa, managing to pick out the flecks of dust that floated in the room, and to make the darkness darker by contrast. The man approached her desk. He had an attaché case in his left hand and placed his right on the back of the bentwood chair that faced the colonel.

"Colonel Vitsin, may I sit?"

"What do you want, Babanin?"

His eyes became abstracted and his smile slightly sickly.

"Colonel, I come with a message from the president." His eyes focused on her. "If you refuse me a seat, you refuse the president a seat."

"Sit." He pulled out the chair and sat. "What do you want, Oleg?"

"After all," he simpered, "courtesy costs nothing."

She leaned forward. Instinctively her right hand reached for her cigarettes. "For me it is a great effort. Now, for the third time, Oleg, what do you want?"

His small, pink lips pinched into a smile. "The president has asked me to speak to you, Alexandrina. 'Oleg, my friend,' he said—this is how he addresses me. 'Oleg, my friend, I am worried about the situation in Spain. I am worried about Alexandrina.'" He wiggled his backside in the chair and giggled. "Of course I said to him, 'Oh, Mr. President, surely Alexandrina is a most capable and experienced operator. She is a great asset and a most valuable member of the intelligence department.' He listens to me, you know, Alexandrina. He pays attention to my advice. 'Do you really believe so, my dear friend Oleg? You know I trust your advice.' I told him, 'She would be almost impossible to replace...'"

He sat smiling at the colonel. There was no expression on her face. The cigarette in her hand trailed smoke, half-obscuring her face and making her squint. Oleg Babanin, ill-concealing his amusement, shifted his gaze to the floor and continued.

"The president said to me, 'Oleg, go and talk to Vitsin, get a full report from her on what is happening in Spain. I do not believe that she is keeping me fully informed. I want America dragged into that war. I do not want to get dragged into a war with America.' He said this most forcefully. So, I am requesting of you, Colonel Vitsin, a *full* report of the progress and objectives of your operation in Spain."

Colonel Vitsin placed the cigarette between her lips and sucked so that the tip glowed red. She opened her mouth and drew the smoke deep into her lungs, then released it in puffs as she spoke.

"You are telling me, Oleg, that you want to take my project from my hands and assume control of it yourself."

"No, no, Colonel Vitsin, nothing could be further from the truth! The president has said to me—"

"You will become the intermediary between me and the president. You will add and subtract from my reports, so that the president gets only what you want him to hear, until you control my operation. This operation that will break the United States and NATO and make Russia the major super-power of the world. This operation which I have been designing and preparing for ten years, you will mince in, with your fat legs and your little gay feet, with your little pink lips, and *steal from me so that you can crawl, sniveling and simpering between the president's buttocks to kiss his ass?*"

Her voice had become shrill at the end. But now she crushed her cigarette and her face creased into a cruel smile, whereupon she threw back her head and laughed out loud. Oleg Babanin watched her with wide, moist eyes.

Her laughter stopped abruptly, but the cruel, nicotine-stained smile lingered on her lips.

"Oleg, my friend, how many years have we known each other? Thirty years? More? You know I have always had the greatest respect for you, and for what you have achieved. You are a subtle, intelligent man and you have known how to deal with your opponents and your enemies." She paused and allowed the smile to fade by just a couple of degrees. "I have been watching you for years. Please, pay no attention to my jokes. I was merely joking. We in Military Intelligence develop a strange sense of humor over the years."

Oleg managed an uncomfortable smile. "Of course."

"Naturally I will have my report ready for you by tomorrow morning. I hope that will be satisfactory."

"Of course, Alexandrina. I hope I have not offended you with my own foolish jokes. You may rest assured that I have nothing but the greatest praise for you when I speak to the president. We can, as ever, be of great help to each other, you and I."

"Tomorrow morning, Oleg."

He nodded, rose and left on hurried little feet.

Once he had carefully closed the door she pulled open a drawer, extracted a cell phone and dialed. After a moment she said:

"I need a report."

"Mason is here. We have traced his credentials as you said, but it seems he is CIA, we can find no connection with any other agency. We are monitoring his communications, and we are monitoring communications in Virginia and in DC."

"His story is that he represents a consortium wishing to invest in Spanish oil, correct?"

"Correct. We have planted a girl and she is getting close to him. We should have something from her soon."

"Soon is not soon enough. Pressure him. You will give

him nothing unless he is willing to bring at least one principal from the consortium. Tell the girl to press him on this. She has been privy to conversations. You are intransigent. Unless his principals come to meet the Andalusian government, you will deal with no one but Russia, Iran and the Arab states. Tell her to convey that. Tell her her life depends on it."

"Yes, Colonel."

She hung up, then picked up the office phone and dialed a single number. After a moment she said, "Secretary Oleg Babanin has been to see me. He had instructions from the president to prepare a report on the status and objectives of the operation in Spain. I have told him the report will be ready for him tomorrow morning. See to it."

And she hung up.

———

OLEG BABANIN RETURNED to his office in the Kremlin. It was a small office with just a desk and a filing cabinet, and no windows. That did not trouble him. As he had told Colonel Vitsin, he did not like windows. Doors were a necessary evil, but for windows he saw no necessity at all. What pleased him, what had given him so much joy he had rushed home and told his mother, was that the office was actually inside the Kremlin. Mama had been so proud of him. She had cooked him a special meal and baked him a cake. That had been a very special day.

His increasingly regular meetings with the president had also pleased Mama. At first she had not believed him, and scolded him for lying, but when he had shown her the memos requiring his presence in the president's office, she had been so impressed she had wept and hugged him. Now, if he could just pull off his own, private operation, if he could persuade Vitsin to let him intercede on her behalf with the president, his status in the Kremlin intelligence network would be fixed in stone, and Mama would be so, so proud of him. He would finally fulfill all her dreams.

He smiled to himself as he boarded the bus and took his seat. He could have a car. He could certainly afford one, and some colleagues had said that in his position he had a duty to wear expensive clothes and drive a BMW or an Audi. He was after all an employee not only of the Russian state, but of the Kremlin. He did not share their view.

He was a communist, a true, loyal communist and he believed still in the Soviet Union, as he knew the president did. And if a Russian bus was good enough for a Russian street cleaner or a Russian factory worker, then it was good enough for him. Of course if the president traveled by bus, or the foreign minister, then that would bring ridicule on the country as a whole.

But he, Oleg Babanin, was not the public face of Russia. He was a small, anonymous man who kept to the shadows, a man nobody noticed, and nobody should notice.

He climbed down from the bus at Delegatskaya Ulitsa as dusk was turning to evening and the streetlamps and car headlamps were coming on. He clutched his attaché case firmly in his left hand, fixed his gaze on the sidewalk seven feet ahead of him, believing firmly that in this attitude he acquired near invisibility, and walked at a steady pace through the trees and into the anonymous, gray, Soviet-era apartment block. The block was fifteen stories high, and he lived on the seventh floor.

There the elevator stopped with a clunk and a rattle. The door jammed, as it always did, halfway open, but yielded to a slight push and he stepped out onto the beige landing. He opened the door with his key, stepped in and turned to close it carefully and called out, "*Zdravstvuy, mama, ya doma!*"

She didn't reply, but he could hear the television playing softly in the living room. He would drop his things in his bedroom, then go and give her a kiss and say hello. She would be pleased to see him.

He glanced at his watch as he moved down the corridor. He was half an hour late and she would probably scold him first, and when he explained that he had been in a meeting with the president, she would then hug him and kiss him, and tell him to sit while she made him his supper.

He opened his bedroom door and stood motionless, frowning. The room was as he had left it at six o'clock that morning, except that his desk, at the foot of his bed, was different. His computer was switched on and on the screen there was a video which had been paused. It displayed a grotesque, nauseating image of a group of soldiers raping a man in a filthy warehouse. And on the desk there were filthy magazines showing men in nauseating positions. He made an inarticulate noise of distress and stepped away from the door.

His mind began to race. Who had done this? This question exploded inside him, his head began to pound, his heart raced and he felt sick. Somebody had been in the apartment.

"Mama! *Mama!*"

He dropped the attaché case and ran back down the

corridor. He burst through the door into the living room, shouting, "*Mama! Mama!*"

And there he stopped, frozen. The television was on. Somebody said something and there was canned laughter. Behind his mother there was a man, looking at him. He had no expression on his face. It was a hard face, as though it were made of stone. His eyes were small and unfeeling. He had his hands on Mama's shoulders. The hands were inside latex gloves. Bizarrely, he noticed the flattened hairs on the fingers, and the fingernails.

His mother was a strange purple color. She was barely recognizable. Her tongue, grotesquely swollen and blue, protruded from her mouth. Her face, blotched blue and purple, was like a balloon, and her eyes. The eyes were horrific, bulging, unhuman.

He felt a movement behind him. A plastic hand took hold of his and he felt the heavy butt of a semi-automatic in his own hand. He felt a firm grip on his elbow and his hand was raised toward his head. A terrible sadness invaded him. A terrible emptiness that seemed to drain away all meaning from his life. He felt tears spill from his eyes and knew what was coming next. He didn't care. When meaning goes, there is nothing else.

Then there was a hard smack, and nothing else.

———

ALEXANDRINA VITSIN DID NOT GO HOME. She had no Mama, no Papochka waiting at home. She had a sofa bed in her office and slept there, when she needed to sleep. She stood at her window, looking down at the dark, empty street, touched here and there by the dull glow of street-lamps, and she smoked, dragging the unfiltered smoke deep into her lungs, holding it and letting it go slowly, controlling it, taking possession of it.

Sometimes she wondered about lung cancer, but on some basic, primal level she believed that she and any cancers that might grow in her system were one and the same being, and they would do her no harm.

It was an idle, amusing thought while she waited for the call. It must come soon, in a few minutes.

The telephone jangled and she smiled, took another drag and walked slowly to the phone. She lifted the receiver.

"Colonel Vitsin speaking."

"This is Maksim Lenkov, personal secretary to the president."

"Good evening, Mr. Lenkov, how can I help you?"

"I am sorry to trouble you so late, Colonel, but I must inform you that Secretary Oleg Babanin has committed suicide this evening at his home."

"I am very sorry to hear that. He was a very capable man. Suicide? Are you sure?"

"There seems very little doubt. He was due to have a meeting with the president tomorrow morning at ten to discuss the situation in Spain. As Mr. Babanin can no longer make it, he requires you to come in his place."

"Please tell the president it will be a great honor for me. I will be there at ten tomorrow. Good night."

"Good night, Colonel."

She replaced the receiver and smiled. Oleg, she had never felt anything but contempt for him. He was cleverer than most, but he had always believed himself far more subtle and intelligent than he in fact was. He had triumphed on others' stupidity rather than his own intelligence. Years ago, when they had played chess together, he had never been more than three moves ahead. She, Alexandrina, was never less than ten moves ahead, and when she contemplated the world situation she was aware that her mind would expand and become vast in three dimensions, and she could think years ahead, contemplating hundreds of moves as though she were observing a gigantic, global chessboard. When she planned, she planned sometimes decades in advance.

And now one of those plans was coming to fruition.

A plan she had been nursing since Victoria Island in the Gulf of Bombay. A plan of vengeance.

NINE

THE MAN KNOWN SIMPLY AS NERO SAT AND drummed his fingers. Patience was one of his great virtues, but right then his virtue was running dry. All cases were supremely important and he treated each case as though it was the most important of his career. But this time it was true. This case could have repercussions so far reaching they defied even his colossal intellect.

And all he could do was sit and try not to stare at the telephone.

He kept turning what few facts he had over in his head, and he kept coming up against the same conclusion: if the worst of his fears were correct, based on his latest information, he had sent Mason into a death trap, and he could not contact him to alert him of the danger without aggravating the situation because, somehow, in some way he could not yet explain, it seemed Russia was eavesdropping on ODIN's communications. The signs were there.

Information he had planted, that was known only to

him and a small group of people, had surfaced in communications intercepted between Moscow and Iran, and more recently between Moscow and her contacts in Spain and the new republic. It was unthinkable that software existed capable of unscrambling and decoding ODIN's electronic messages. Which left only one option, that somebody within ODIN had made the deciphering codes available to Moscow.

A lockdown on all communication was impossible, not least because it would alert the Russians to the fact that the leak had been noticed. That meant that all but the most sensitive communication must continue while they tracked down the source of the leak. And meanwhile communication with Mason was all but paralyzed.

In a sudden savage act he pounded his fist on the desk and bellowed, "*Lovelock!*"

Her voice oozed back, like a particularly pleasant sin. "Yes, sir?"

"*Oysters, god dammit! And Dom Pérignon!*"

"The good one, sir?"

"*No! Confound it! I am not celebrating!*" And then, more quietly, "I am drowning my sorrows."

"Yes sir."

Five minutes later Lovelock entered his office and found him staring sullenly at the telephone. She placed a bucket of ice on his desk and put a plate with a dozen oysters on it in front of him. Beside it she placed a frosted glass. While she set to work opening the bottle he looked first at the oysters and then at her.

"To look at me, Lovelock, you would not think I am a man of action."

"Someone who didn't know you."

"You know me well by now, I think. You know that my mind never stops, and I *make things happen!*" He clenched his fist as he said it.

The bottle popped and she spilled the wine into the glass. He eyed her as the foam settled.

"Things have not been so precarious, Lovelock, there has not been so much at stake, since 1939."

The foam died away and Lovelock filled the glass to just above halfway.

"I think you mean 1936."

His head snapped round and he stared up at her. Then, for the first time in weeks his face cracked into a smile and he began to laugh. "Yes!" He said, "Yes indeed! Very good Lovelock, 1936. In Spain. If Franco had been stopped, who knows what would have happened to Hitler and Mussolini."

The smile slipped from his face and he stared down at the oysters. Lovelock spoke quietly. "Any word from Mason?"

"Nothing!" he said savagely. "Not a word."

"Can I get you anything else?"

He shook his huge head. "Nothing."

In a strangely intimate gesture she touched his shoulder with her fingertips. He seemed not to notice and she left.

That was when the phone rang. Not the office phone but the phone they had set aside for alleged communication with the investment consortium. It stopped ringing and after a moment Lovelock's voice came over the intercom.

"Mr. Branson, it's Mr. Mason on line one, calling from Malaga."

Nero snatched up the telephone. "Alex," he said in a

voice that suggested he might be reading the paper while he spoke. "What news?"

"Not much, sir. To tell you the truth, I think I am getting the runaround."

"In what sense, Alex?"

"Well, for a start, I have been shown the oil field at Baza, which is very impressive and is making remarkable progress, and the really pretty huge field they have next door, which Dr. Montilla tells me is full of what he called plant: machinery, equipment, all that kind of stuff, under sage green tents."

"Yes, I understand."

"But when I asked how we, the US, could help, he made two things very clear to me. What they most want from us is international recognition as an independent republic, and in the second place they are getting everything they need in terms of software, hardware, expertise and training from the Russians and, especially in terms of boots on the ground, the Iranians."

"Boots..."

"Yes, expert training in laying pipelines, people with all the appropriate training and experience."

"I understand."

"When I met with the Minister for Oil, sir, he told me something interesting. They are interested in American money, but before they were willing to negotiate with me they wanted more proof of who I was. They seem to suspect I am working for the CIA."

"The CIA could never afford you."

"Ha! I guess that's true. In any case, what he told me was

that he would want to negotiate directly with at least one of the consortium's principals."

"Where are you now?"

"At the portal of hell, in a place called Baza. The consolation is my guide seems to have been planted to elicit pillow talk from me. I think I might let her."

"Vulgar, Alex. Always vulgar and facetious."

"Also, one day you should come and see this place. It is a clay desert where people still live in caves. Only the angel Gabriel's daughter would come here."

"Crude but effective. We live in desperate times."

He hung up.

So, Gabriel's daughter, Aila Gallin was there. Naturally the Mossad would be deeply concerned at Iran's acquiring a foothold inside Europe and NATO. Especially with the backing of Russia.

But it was the rest of the message that worried him. He took an oyster and swallowed it, then sipped at the champagne. The door opened and Lovelock leaned on the jamb, looking at him.

"Aila is there," he said.

"That's to be expected."

"Yes, the Mossad will be extremely worried. Who could have predicted this?"

She moved into the office and sat on the edge of his desk. "It has all the hallmarks of having been planned over a very long time. This isn't Putin. This is someone behind Putin, someone who bears the scars of the Soviet Union and wants revenge."

"I agree. This is revenge, not just for the Ukraine, but for Afghanistan too." He took another oyster and gestured at the plate. Lovelock reached down and took one. She swallowed it and sipped from his glass.

"He tells me there is a large military camp beside the Baza well. It is disguised and they are claiming it is material for building the wells."

She nodded. "That's what showed on the satellite pictures."

"Yes, but what concerns me most is that they are telling him they need nothing from us. Russia and Iran are providing them with all the material and logistical help they need, including, as he said, boots on the ground. He used the term referring to experts in the construction of pipelines, but any native speaker knows that boots on the ground refers to soldiers."

"Bluff? Negotiating from strength?"

"Possibly. They told him they would not consider any kind of negotiation with his consortium unless they met at least one of the principals in person. They believe that he works for the CIA."

She was quiet, watching him as he worked his way through three more oysters. Finally she said, "Who will you send?"

He studied her for a long moment. "I am not sure," he said at last. "I need to think this through."

She reached down and picked up another oyster. He watched her swallow it and sip from his glass again. As he took the glass from her he said, "Mitch York."

She pouted at the ceiling. "Interesting... CEO of Universal Investments Inc. with its head office in Panama, on the boards of several other investment banks, advisor to the president on energy issues and intelligence, a known hawk where fossil fuels are concerned, believes climate change is a liberal conspiracy, and has been lobbying for an invasion of Iran for the last ten years, governor of Arizona."

Nero held up his hand. "He's our man. Get him for me and I'll brief him on what's needed."

She took the last oyster, swallowed it and drained his glass before refilling it. She stood and gave him a lopsided smile.

"He and Aila should get on like a house on fire."

TEN

GALLIN NARROWED HER EYES AND SUCKED ON HER teeth like she had just recently had a steak. Not many people can make that look good, but Gallin pulled it off.

"Alex Mason, huh? I imagined you older and more...," she placed her hands like she was holding a large drum, "corpulent."

"I'm surprised you've imagined me at all. Is there any reason why you would?"

"Colleagues," she said unhelpfully. "Ira Levin, you remember Ira?" I made a noncommittal face and damned her to hell silently behind a pleasant smile. "He remembers you. He said you were a giant in the world of finance. 'He's a giant, Aila, a giant among me,'" she added, making a decent job of turning a stereotype into an archetype, "'I knew him when he was a boy. Now he's a man. It happens. A giant. Or maybe that was his father.' He had Alzheimer's, so he wasn't sure. But I got the impression you were, you know, kind of corpulent. Do you think Alois Alzheimer remembered that he had identified presenile dementia?"

While I took a moment to frown Gallin turned to Ana. "Hi, are you his keeper? He's a kind of lesser god in Israel. I haven't much time for lesser gods. If you're going to be a god, be a major one, right. His superpower is negotiating. He's a real badass at negotiating."

Ana smiled politely, the way people smile politely when a drunk stranger sways up and starts talking in a foreign language. I turned back to Dr. Montilla who was ogling Gallin's legs with almost professional concentration.

"Doctor, has every drilling site got a comparable storage yard beside it, like this one?"

He nodded at Gallin's ass and then frowned at me. "Eh? Yard? Oh, yet, pretty much, kind of."

Gallin added, "Because as soon as you get a hit, you want the materials at hand to start exploiting the well, right?"

"That is correct, yes."

She slipped her arm around his shoulder, leaned in close and pointed, breathing softly in his ear.

"Do you have personnel down there? They look like tents."

"Some," he said in a surprisingly deep voice and cleared his throat. "Not, no, not really, a few—"

"Security guards, suchlike—"

"Yuh, exactly, kind of thing."

We killed an hour or two examining a couple of the rigs. Dr. Montilla told us no oil had been struck yet because the deposits had been found at exceptional depths which, until that time, had been undetectable and un-extractable, but they expected their first strike in the next few days, and after that extraction would begin in earnest thanks to the new, Russian technology.

Lunch in this part of the world is taken, in a leisurely fashion, at about three in the afternoon, when the sun is at its most unforgiving, and is followed by a couple of hours of siesta. By half past two we had been at the field for more than two hours, my brain was telling me there was not much to be seen without getting myself shot, and my belly was telling me lunchtime had been and gone without food, and what was I going to do about it?

So I thanked Dr Montilla, told Ana I thought it was time we went and had lunch and turned to Gallin.

"Where are you staying?"

"Only one place in town, Mason, the Anabel."

"You need a ride?"

"I always have my own ride, Mason. But thanks, anyhow."

"Well, in that case, maybe you'd like to dine with us tonight?"

"Oh, I'd love that." As I turned to follow Ana, I heard Gallin behind me, "Catch you tonight, big guy."

We found a place in the shade to park outside the hotel and I told Ana to go in, grab a table and order me a cold beer. While she did that I took a stroll down the road to the *Plaza de las Eras*. I made like a tourist and looked at every-thing everywhere, and saw I was not being followed. At three PM in Baza, with the thermometer about to burst at a hundred and twenty F, there was no one in the street, not even mad dogs and Englishmen. I pulled out one of the burners I had bought and called Nero.

"I hope you have some news for me. I don't think I can eat many more oysters."

"Yeah? I troubles me that I know what you mean. That statement shouldn't make any sense. I have news for you."

I put him up to date and told him the Minister for Oil wanted to meet at least one of my principals. Then I told him about the Baza oil fields and the military encampments. When I'd finished he made a sound like he'd started thinking about oysters again.

"This is not a good situation, Alex. This is not good, however you view it."

"I'd have to agree."

"Are you being facetious? I can't tell."

"No, I'd say that, on the face of it, that Andalusian government seems to be hell-bent on provoking Spain into a civil war. I'd say they are pushing for a flashpoint, and when that comes they are going to deploy Russian arms and Iranian troops."

"I agree. That causes a very large problem for us. Let me think. I'll be in touch. I'll call you on this number, then throw the cell away. Destroy it."

"Are you going to send someone?"

"I don't know. We are leaking. That complicates things. I'll call you."

I hung up and made my way back to the hotel.

At the hotel I found Gallin in the lounge watching TV. She was alone in there and she'd set the TV to the BBC. I went in and she glanced at me without saying anything, then looked back at the screen. There was a guy in a sweatshirt standing outside the Moncloa Palace in Madrid, holding a microphone and talking to the camera.

"...behind me diplomacy has reached fever pitch. Mr Biden, the president of the United States, has been locked in with Alvaro Romero for the last three hours trying to negotiate some kind of deal. But as Romero stated to the entire Spanish nation shortly before meeting the president of the United States, 'What kind of deal can you make with people who enlist foreign forces to tear your country apart?' I understand that Mr. Biden will appeal to Mr. Romero on behalf of all Western leaders to back away from war. How much weight the American president will carry is a moot point, as Mr. Romero has stated repeatedly that he has not sought a conflict with Andalusia or with Russia, but Benjamin Musa and Mr. Putin have sought a fight with him. In his own words to us just three hours ago—"

They cut to a scene outside the parliament building, the *Palacio de las Cortes* where the acting president had a number of microphones shoved in his face. He was talking as he walked down the steps to a waiting limo.

'What am I to do? They murder my president and my closest friend, they tear my country in half and try to cripple it economically, and I am supposed to show restraint? Too much! Too much restraint I have shown already! The Spanish people are shouting for justice. Shall I fail them? Shall I betray them like has done Benjamin Musa? No, not me."

I sat in the vinyl chair beside Gallin, with a lamp table between us. It squeaked but she ignored me and the scene changed back to the BBC reporter outside the Moncloa.

"I am just five hundred yards from the very place where Jesus Sanchez was so recently gunned down. As yet no clue has emerged as to the identity of the gunmen, despite the cooperation of international intelligence services and the offer of the American government to put the cutting-edge technology of their laboratories at the service of the Spanish government. There are, however, rumors filtering out from the SIC, the Spanish Intelligence Community, that the gunmen who shot down Jesus Sanchez were Middle Eastern. That is, as I say, little more than rumor, and allegedly the personal opinion of one of the lead investigators."

Gallin picked up the remote control on the table in front of her and killed the TV.

"Hello Mr. Mason. I thought you were desperate for lunch? Your beautiful companion has gone up to her room."

"Hello, Captain Gallin. I had something to attend to, I shall lunch presently."

"Not many men are brave enough to use lunch as a verb these days."

"Your legs, even encased in denim as they are, are enough to make a hero of the most rank coward."

She arched an eyebrow at me. "That should be nauseating, and yet..."

"I will go to Malaga. What about you? Same. I'm at the Marriott Malaga Palace."

She nodded and shrugged. "Where else? It wouldn't be smart for us to be seen socializing. You got a burner?"

I gave her a number and watched her face go blank while she memorized it. Then she said, "You going to go in and look at the military bases?"

I felt a sudden, hot burn of anxiety in my belly. "That's not my brief so far. Are you?"

"I need to know if it's true the Iranians are putting in weapons and men."

"There may be a safer way to do that."

"Are you worried for me, Mr. Mason? That would be most unprofessional."

"Quit horsing around. Is that your plan?"

"I don't know. You'd better go and have lunch. Your Spanish beauty will be getting antsy."

I stood and made my way to the door. There I stopped and looked back at her. There was something like a smile on her lips, and something that might have been hopeful in her eyes. I said, "We tried to get ourselves killed together so many times, it would be a shame if, you know..." I trailed off.

"If I got killed one place, some time, somehow, and you got killed some other place, time and how?"

I nodded. "That."

"Don't worry. If I ever aim to get killed I'll make sure and send you an invite."

"That's mighty big of you, ma'am."

I went to look for my Spanish beauty. She was in her room, next to mine, freshly showered and freshly beautiful. She cocked her head at me, smiled like an ad for hair product, took my arm and led me down the stairs again to the dining room. As we sat she asked me, "Who's your friend?"

"Which one in particular?" I asked, which was a mistake because it told her I was being evasive. She arched an eyebrow. "The only one I have met?"

"You mean Captain Gallin. She's not really a friend. Our paths have crossed occasionally, similar line of work."

"Really? I thought you were a government agent involved in counterespionage. That's what your boss told me anyhow. Is that what Captain Gallin does too?"

I gave her the blandest of my smiles. "Not that I am

aware of, Ana. But you'd be amazed at how much cloak and dagger business goes on in Middle Eastern oil. As far as I know she was in the Israeli army, like most Israelis, and then moved into petrochemicals and oil. In any case, she is not a friend, just an acquaintance. Why do you ask?"

The waiter had arrived with the menus, and I ordered her a martini and for myself the cold beer I had been dreaming about. When he'd gone away with our orders she shrugged and pulled down the corners of her mouth.

"Simple curiosity. She is very beautiful. I think she would like to know you better."

I made a face like I had bigger things on my mind than some crazy broad who wanted to have my kids and introduce me to her parents.

She wasn't fooled but we both looked at the menu in silence for a bit. Finally she ordered grilled prawns from Huelva followed by a fish they called rape, in Roman style, which did not involve the rapid removal of togas, but turned out to be battered monkfish. I had a small, sizzling terracotta dish of spicy prawns followed by grilled kid, and when we were sitting over the last of the wine my cell rang again.

"Mr. Mason." It was Nero, the only person it could be.

"Good afternoon, Mr. Brown. How are you this afternoon?"

"It is not afternoon yet, Mr. Mason. However, as you ask, I am the better for having had a dish of oysters and a bottle of Dom Perignon. I understand the Andalusian government is anxious to meet at least one member of the board of investors here."

I looked at Ana, winked and nodded. "Yes, sir, they are understandably worried that this may be little more than a fishing expedition to see how things are likely to develop in the future, once they settle down."

"That is understandable."

"Eminently. Has anybody offered to come over?"

"Mitch York."

"Well, if nothing else he should put some minds at rest. Straight talking, shoots from the hip," I looked at Ana and nodded, "CEO of Universal Investments, on the boards of four investment banks, advisor to the president on energy and intelligence. He is something of a hawk where fossil fuels are concerned, is known to be a climate change denier, and has been lobbying for an invasion of Iran for the last ten years. Governor of Arizona."

He was quiet for a long moment. "How much to do you and Lovelock speak in my absence, Alex?"

"Hardly at all, sir. Why?"

"Mr. York will be arriving at Malaga Airport in about twenty-four hours, by private jet. Be sure to take him to your hotel and debrief him, in particular with regard to the SU-22 Russian fighter-bombers you reported you had seen near Baza. I need hardly say that this information is of the highest sensitivity and is, as of this moment, known only to you and me. Tomorrow, Mitch will make three."

"OK, I will make sure he has a great time while he's here. No worries there, sir."

He told me the suite York would be staying in and added, "Keep me posted."

Ana made a question with her face. I said, "Mitch York is coming over to meet Don Manuel Torreras Carbonell, your Minister for Oil. With a bit of luck that should ease things up a bit."

"How?" There was just a touch of a challenge in her eyes.

I pretended not to notice, but leaned forward and sipped my wine. "Well, if you have American corporations courting your oil and offering you billions of dollars if you'll just play ball, what would you do, cozy up with the Russians and the Iranians, or play ball with Uncle Sam? Cooperate with Uncle Sam and you stay inside Europe and inside NATO. Nobody gets shot."

She shook her head. "The problem with you Americans is always the same. You think everybody is crazy to get your dollars. Sometimes things are more important than dollars: freedom, dignity, self-determination. I am not here with you now because I want Spain to buy Coca-Cola and McDonald's and Levi's Jeans, and be another little colony for the latest big empire. I am here because I do not want Spain to divide, to be taken over by Russia and allow Iran to bring Sharia law to this country, and turn the women into slaves for the men."

I watched her a moment and wondered. Sometimes the same passions that can make you the most loyal ally, even unto death, can make you the most treacherous enemy with the slightest shift of perspective.

"I agree with you, Ana. I am not here to sell you McDonald's and Coca-Cola. I am here to help you save your country, and avoid a major war."

"I hope so," she said. "I really hope so."

I hoped so too.

ELEVEN

About halfway through dinner a man came in on short legs. He had a jacket that hung down to his knees, dusty plastic shoes and an ill-concealed weapon under his arm. He sat at a table in the corner and carefully ignored us while he ate a garbanzo and chorizo stew with hunks of bread, and drank Coke.

Just after he'd come in and sat down, Ana reached across the table and held my hand. There was a terrible sadness in her eyes.

"I have to get close to you."

I smiled. "You can always put a paper bag over my head and close your eyes."

She didn't smile. "That is not really funny, Alex."

"Keep going like that and the little bald guy with the badly cut suit is going to get worried."

"You want me to laugh?" There was a bitter twist in her dark eyes.

I laughed like she's said something amusing, raised her

hand to my lips and kissed her fingers. "I'd like you to get to next week alive, if that's at all possible."

"Why?"

"Because, even though you are way too serious, and you had obviously popped to the ladies when they were handing out senses of humor, I kind of like you."

Her brow contracted slightly. "You like me?"

"Yeah, there's a kind of urgent sincerity to you which is quite likeable."

I turned toward the windows, and the few people gathered in the dining room looked up from their meals to watch the flashing red and blue lights cruise by; all but the guy in the badly cut suit. He stayed focused on his garbanzo beans.

The waiter, standing in the middle of the floor holding a tray, said to nobody in particular, "*Toque de queda*."

Ana said quietly, "Curfew," then she turned her eyes on me. "It is not that long ago that we had curfews in Spain. My grandparents lived through that, even after the war. It came with the knock on the door at four in the morning. The Guardia Civil would come to your house, take you away and you were never seen again. Two hundred and fifty thousand people died after the war, more than in the three years that the war lasted, executed in the orchards and the fields. They would take them during the curfew, out into the country, cut their bonds and tell them, 'Go on, run, we don't want to kill you,' and as they ran away they would shoot them in the back. All of this is coming back now."

Tears had welled in her eyes, but had not spilled yet. She hadn't let go of my hand yet. I cupped hers in both of mine and squeezed it.

"I can't imagine what that was like, and I can't imagine

what it's like to have your home balanced on the brink of war. But I do know this, Ana. You're a pro, like me. And as pros we cannot allow ourselves to sink into depression and negativity. We have to do what we can to pull Spain back from the abyss."

"One man, and an incompetent girl? Do you know what I was doing six months ago?"

"I'm not interested."

"I was an office girl, filing documents in the civil service. Now I am a spy and a whore for a puppet government controlled by the Russians and radical Islam."

I leaned forward across the table, leaning on my elbows, and pulled her closer to me. Her eyes were turning wild. I smiled and whispered, "You had better start getting cozy and affectionate with me, kiddo, or Baldy and his friends are going to be knocking on your door at four in the morning to take you out to the orchard." I kissed her hand again and smiled. "Get serious, Ana. You are playing a very dangerous game right now."

I leaned back in my chair and signaled the waiter. To Ana I said, "We are going to have a drink, then we are going to go up to my room. There, you can sleep on the bed and I will sleep on the floor. But that will be our naughty secret."

She had a cognac and I had a whisky.

"Six months ago you were filing papers. Just a few, short years ago I was searching for lost civilizations."

She arched both her eyebrows, the anger suddenly gone from her face. "Doing what?"

"Searching for lost civilizations in the Bay of Bengal."

She threw back her head and laughed. I glanced at the

man with the long jacket and the short legs. He was enjoying a private smile. She said, "So you are human, after all."

"Of course. It's a myth that people," I paused a moment, then said with care, "people in my line of work are heartless, soulless monsters. You get the odd one who has buried his humanity, but you get that in all professions, doctors, lawyers, administrators, nuns, priests, charity workers. Sometimes human beings lose their humanity. You know one of the weirdest things I ever saw?"

She was smiling. "I can't imagine."

The memory made me frown. "It's a memory that haunts me, but I never want to lose it because it's a north star, it reminds me of what I never want to become. I was in —a country in the Middle East—to..."

"Negotiate a contract for oil?"

I gave her a lopsided smile. "Exactly that, and I was forced to witness a session of waterboarding. It was horrific. I am not going to make any moral judgment on whether those men should have been tortured that way or not. They had murdered and raped women and children, and it's possible that lives were saved because they were tortured. We can moralize and philosophize till the cows come home, but what it comes down to in the moment is, what are you prepared to do in order to save the next victims' lives?" She didn't say anything. She just stared at me. I went on. "But the thing that really shocked me, because I was pretty new to the business, was the senior CIA officer who was present."

"What shocked you about him? Surely the CIA do this kind of thing routinely. Or don't you know this in—"

I cut her short. "What surprised me, Ana, was the way

he had to rush to the corner and vomit, and then ran outside in tears; a man in his forties with twenty years' experience."

"You expect me to believe that?"

I nodded. "Yup. Because the path to hell starts when we rob *other people* of their humanity. Once *they* stop being human, we can do what the hell we like to them. As long as we allow others to retain their humanity, we retain our own."

I drained my glass while she stared at the table. As I put it down I did a serviceable imitation of Bogart, "Come on, shweetheart, take me upstairs and do what you do besht."

The bedrooms had cute Chubb locks with actual, mechanical keys. I opened the door to my room and let her in. She stopped just behind me as I locked the door, and when I turned she was facing me.

"You are a strange man," she said.

"Yeah, but the surgeon says he can fix that."

"Stop joking, Alex. I am serious. You are not the man I thought you were. When I first met you I hated you, because I associated you with your American empire. But I see now that I was wrong. I see you now as who you are." She came closer and placed her hands on my shoulders. "If I must make love to you, I don't mind. Now, I want to give you my body."

What can I tell you? Sometimes it's just rude to say no.

———

NEXT DAY we headed back to Malaga first thing after breakfast. We didn't talk much, but most of the way she had her hand on my knee. At Guadix she asked me, "How can you go from archeologist to CIA agent, working for a country like the United States?"

"First of all," I told her, "I was an amateur archeologist. I was born to privilege. My family had a lot of money, which I inherited, and I was fascinated by the idea that there might have been an advanced civilization before the end of the Ice Age."

She showed me a "that wasn't my question" face.

"Second, the CIA doesn't have agents. The CIA has officers, and as I explained to you before, there are all sorts of people working for the CIA. Sure, there are departments who employ ex-special forces to conduct assassinations, like Bin Laden, but there are other departments that intercede in situations like this one, to prevent what civilization we have in the West descending into chaos."

I hadn't answered her question, and I had no intention of doing so. What I was wondering was why she had asked it in the first place. Maybe she was the naïve civil servant she claimed to be. And I had to admit that, if she wasn't, she was a damned good actress.

On the other hand, maybe she was a damned good actress who was working as a double agent for Benjamin Musa. If he believed I was CIA, that was fine by me, and she had no need to know there was any other agency taking care of the USA's foreign relations.

I dropped her at the port in Malaga and made my way on out to the airport. I had received a message as we were approaching the city that Mitch York's plane was approaching to land.

All along the coast road, while the United Nations, the European Union and the United States were in frantic discussions with the Spanish government and the internationally unrecognized government of Andalusia, that legally nonexistent government was equally frantically putting up razor wire and gun emplacements all along the beaches from Murcia in the east to Gibraltar in the west. It was a surreal image. I had seen its like many times in the Middle East, but seeing it on the beaches of a European city, which just a few weeks earlier had been an integral part of one of the most stable economic blocks on the planet, was sobering.

And as I followed the road away from the coast, north toward the airport, all the major junctions and circuses had at least one armored car watching the traffic, and as I drew closer to the airport I saw that in the few hours I had been there, they had ringed the entire place with anti-aircraft, ground-to-air missile trucks and gun emplacements, as well as tanks and heavy machine guns. They didn't aim to give up the airport without a fight.

And as I pulled in to arrivals I saw that, where many of the passenger planes had been removed, there were now fighters and fighter-bombers sitting on the tarmac. It was hard to make them out, but I wondered if they were Russian or Iranian.

The main concourse was empty but for soldiers and Guardia Civil. I felt huge and cavernous as I stepped inside and was stopped by a guy in a green uniform with an assault rifle hanging over his shoulder. He snapped, "*Donde va?*" as he blocked my path.

I have some basic Spanish, but I didn't see any reason

why I should make life any easier for a guy with no manners. So I screwed up my face and said, "*Americano, habla ingles, por favor?*"

He turned and I saw his captain approaching on squeaky black jackboots. The grunt muttered something about "*Ingles,*" and his captain jerked his chin at me and said, "Papers!"

I reached in my breast pocket, pulled out my passport and handed it to him. "I am here to meet a plane from Washington DC, a Mr. Mitch York. We have an appointment with *Señor Manuel Torreras Carbonell, ministro de aceite.*"

His eyes scanned the photograph page, then scanned my face. He handed it back and snapped, "Downstairs, in Arrivals."

I gave a meaningless smile. "Thank you, Captain, I'll be sure to mention you to the minister." But my ineffectual barb bounced harmlessly off his hide. He had black, squeaky jackboots now, and he felt invincible.

Arrivals was almost as empty as it was upstairs. In fact there were only the green uniforms with their automatic weapons and Mitch York and his two bodyguards pushing their suitcases through the vast, cavernous hall. They saw me and came toward me, looking fresh and rested. Mitch York had permed silver hair and the kind of jaw you can only get from wrastling broncos and brawling at square dances. He approached saying, "You Mason?"

"Yes, sir."

"Mitch, good to meet you, son. Take me to the nearest martini."

"Nearest place is the hotel. Most of the bars and restaurants are closed. I've got my car waiting upstairs. Good flight?"

We chit-chatted small talk till we were out of the airport and I'd slung the cases in the trunk of the Mustang. We climbed in and slammed the doors and I fired up the big V8. And as we pulled out of the airport he asked me, "You part of Nero's outfit?"

I smiled blandly as they waved us through the checkpoint and onto the highway that led into the city.

"I guess that depends what you mean by Nero's outfit."

"Don't play cute with me, son. I've been in this game since they used stilettos and capes, eh, boys?"

He craned his neck to look at the two hulks in the backseat. I glanced at them in the mirror and saw them nod mechanically. Mitch looked at me and laughed. "Stilettos and capes! Eh? Cloak and dagger. Been in the game since the Cold War, before the wall came down. Shook hands with Reagan, greatest president we ever had. Forget Kennedy, communist son of a bitch, screwing Marilyn Monroe, sharing her with his son of a bitch brother, no personal standards, no integrity. Reagan, Reagan was a man who lived what he stood for."

I let him talk. I figured as long as he was talking he wasn't asking questions.

We had pulled off the highway and were moving down the coast road, so he could see the gun emplacements and the ground-to-air missiles, and he was telling me that despite our historical differences he admired the British because they knew how to wage war. I told him I agreed, and thought to myself it was probably time to take back control of the conversation.

"Speaking of war," I said, as I crossed the main avenue and pulled up outside the hotel, "it seems to me Andalusia is preparing for war." The mention of war had his attention straight away. "Yeah, we pretty much knew that, son. Everybody does."

I shook my head. "Not invasion, war."

TWELVE

I climbed out of the Mustang and addressed the two hulks in the backseat. "You guys want to take the cases inside while I talk to your boss?"

They exchanged a silent look and must have communicated telepathically, because one of them took up a position on the steps just out of earshot, while the other carried the cases inside. When they were gone I turned to York.

"I am not sure if Nero mentioned it, but yesterday I was out at the Baza oil fields."

"He said something."

I put my hand on his shoulder and led him a couple of steps away, talking quietly.

"They are drilling still, and they are going at it with a will. So far they haven't struck anything, but they are confident it is a matter of a few days. Now, what concerned me more was the mile wide—at least—military camp they have set up next door."

He nodded his big, leonine head. "Yeah, we've had some sight of those from the satellites."

"I'm sure you have. They have made no effort to hide them, but with the dust out there, the heat and the camouflage tents I'd be surprised if you got much detail."

"Not much, no. What did you see?"

I gave my head a small twitch. "It was more of a snatched glance, because we were half a mile away or more. I wondered at first if I was meant to see it, but the way they covered it up, I don't think so."

"See what, son?"

"They have powerful desert winds out there, and one gust caught one of the camouflage tarps and whipped it off what at first looked like a large stash of equipment. That's what they'd told us the camp was, an equipment stash. But what I saw under the tarp was a fighter, and I would swear it was an SU-22 Russian fighter-bomber. I tried to make like I hadn't noticed and looked away pretty quick, but when I had another look it seemed to me there must have been at least ten of them lined up."

We talked a little bit more about the details and he made to go back toward the hotel. I said, "What time is your appointment with Torreras? You need a ride?"

He shook his head. "Thanks, no. He's sending a car for me."

I had ditched the burner just outside Malaga, after I'd received the message that York was approaching for landing. Now I took a walk up toward the cathedral and called Nero.

Lovelock answered. "This is six o'clock in the morning Washington DC, how can I make your day special?"

"It might not have been me."

"I didn't think it was. What can I do for you, handsome?"

"You can put me through to Nero, but only after you promise to dine with me. He suspects us, you know?"

"And I bet his suspicions are so much more fun than your reality."

There was a click and a moment's silence, then Nero's unmistakable growl, "Report."

"The doggie is in the pen, the riata is slung and we are hittin' the trail."

His sigh was loud. "Must you? I gather you have met Mitch York, he has arrived without incident and you have given him the information."

"I'm sorry, sir. I thought that was what I'd said."

"If you are attempting to be amusing you are failing. Listen to me. I need you to stand by, Alex. Assimilate this: should I come across your wife again, I shall need you to have serious words with her. Do you understand?"

"Yeah, but I'd need you to confirm how serious."

"No, you wouldn't. And if that circumstance should arise, then I might have to come over myself to talk with Musa."

"That would be a really bad idea, sir."

"I am aware of that, Alex, but sometimes a really bad idea is the only one you have available, and in those cases all you can do is the best that you can."

"I believe that makes sense sir, but only because you said it. If anybody else said it, I'd tell them it was bullshit."

"Don't be insolent. I'll be in touch."

He hung up and left me feeling a little queasy. The thought of all four hundred-and-a-lot of Nero leaving his office and climbing onto a plane was bad enough. The thought of him coming to a country poised on the edge of civil war was beyond words. What if he was arrested? Put in prison and forced to eat garbanzo stew and drink tap water? He'd never survive. I shuddered and made my way back toward the hotel. Some things are too unnatural to even contemplate.

I strolled into the lobby considering the fact that Nero would have said, "even to contemplate," because he would never split his infinitives. With not much else to do right then but consider split infinitives, I thrust my hands in my pockets and made my way toward the bar, where I ordered a Bushmills straight up from a guy with permed hair and a burgundy waistcoat. As I climbed on the stool, over my shoulder I heard a voice that launched a thousand ships, and then sank them. It said:

"Of all the gin joints in all the towns in all the world, he walks into mine."

I turned to look at her as the waiter set down a tumbler and some peanuts in front of me.

"A martini dry for the lady," I told him. She'd changed out of her jeans and khaki and changed into something disturbing. "I was with the *Iliad*," I told her, trying to focus on her deep brown eyes instead of her scarlet, low-cut assault on decency. "And you came in with *Casablanca*."

She climbed on the stool next to mine and crossed her legs. "I was once told by a man with a goatee that erudition can be very debilitating to a man's libido."

I nodded and scratched my chin. "I might agree if I knew

what erudition was. And anyway, the *Iliad* is my least favorite of Stan Lee's movies."

"You know? You're almost funny when you don't mean to be. How was the airport?"

"Do you know how those barbs wound? You'll have to make it up to me one day, and heal all those scars in my heart. The airport had more tanks and ground-to-air missiles than airplanes. So I am told."

"Who's your friend with the concrete, silver hair and the pseudo military air?"

"Why don't you ask your daddy? Did I mention you look disturbing?"

"He asked me to ask you. I caught sight of myself in the mirror before coming down. If I were a narcissist I would date myself. But I am not so instead I wondered if you would desire me."

"I do, intensely, but you seem so unattainable in that dress."

"He reminded me a lot of Mitch York. Which made me wonder why anybody would want to send Mitch York to Andalusia right now, on the brink of civil war. Would it make me seem more attainable if I took the dress off, Alex?"

I downed half my whiskey, sighed warmly and smacked my lips like I was thinking. "I think that would be a general improvement all round, but I would not recommend it in the bar."

The waiter placed her drink in front of her. She smiled and leaned in close to me with her hand on my knee.

"I'll tell you what we'll do, handsome. The silver fox has just crossed the lobby with a guy in a dark suit and a peaked cap, and he is climbing into an official-looking car. I am going to tail him inconspicuously, like only we know how. And meanwhile you sit here and attract attention as an oil investor." She leaned closer so her lips brushed my ear. "And later tonight, when you have ditched your little minder, come to my room, I will remove my dress, so that you don't feel I am unattainable, and tell you what I have learned, and in return you can tell me all about Mr. York and why he is here."

She breathed warmly on my ear, slipped off the stool and walked out, leaving her martini untouched. Sometimes life is just all about the things you can't have.

I thought about tailing Gallin, but decided it was unnecessary on several scores, the most important of which was that I knew where York was going. He was going to see Manuel Torreras, the Andalusian Minister for Oil. Plus, ODIN, and the security services of the Five Eyes nations that constituted it, had a pretty solid understanding with the Mossad. However soft politicians might feel it was expedient to get on Islam, the guys at the front line kept talking to each other. The basic equation behind the arrangement was that by and large too many good soldiers get shot, and too few politicians.

So, even if I was wrong and York was not going to see Torreras, Gallin was willing to trade information. She had intimated as much when she'd told me her father had told her to ask me why York was there. Her father was the director of the London field office of the Mossad, and he was offering to collaborate. Collaborating with the Mossad was rarely a waste of time.

I went to my suite and selected one of my few remaining burners. With it I called a number in Antequera, about an hour inland from Malaga city, in the mountains. It rang four times before a Cockney voice said, "What?"

"Is that the NRA?"

"That would be almost funny if it wasn't so fuckin' stupid. Who is this?"

"Bert, why do you Brits swear so much? Are you unable to articulate a simple idea without interlacing it with expletives?"

"No, we fuckin' can't. Next question, what do you want you Yankee tosser?"

"I am over here in Spain, enjoying the tense atmosphere of imminent conflagration, and thought maybe we could have a beer."

"No way mate, we are under curfew, in case you hadn't noticed. I can't go beyond walking distance."

"But I can, because I am an American billionaire interested in furthering the cause of Andalusian independence and American imperialism."

"You fuckin' bastard."

"Wrong, Bert. I am assured my parents were married when I was born, or at least very shortly after, though not necessarily to each other. Where shall we meet by accident?"

"Bar *La Perdiz*, in the *Plaza Espíritu Santo*. It's in a square which is a triangle, there are steps up to a fountain, and the bar, which is called the Partridge, don't have a picture of a fahkin' partridge hanging over the door, coz that would be too easy, wouldn't it? Instead it's got a picture of a fat geezer dressed in red, like a fahkin' tart, drinking a pint of what passes for beer over here. See? That's why they lost their bleedin' empire. Coz they don't think logically. It's a fahkin' partridge, not a fahkin' fat bloke—"

"Bert. You hate this place, why do you live here?"

"It's the weather, innit? Also, if I go home I'll go to prison for the rest of me life. What do you want?"

"You know me preference is what you call a quiet Sam Smith, double and half again. I don't want a Google Lock."

"Single use, or you gonna keep it?"

"Disposable."

"Today?"

"Yeah. In a couple of hours."

"Can you find me?"

"Of course."

"Right, see you then."

I hung up. Since 9/11 it has been very difficult for people in my profession to carry weapons from one country to another. So, fairly quickly, a whole new market opened up for illicit, but protected, small arms dealers all over the world. Some operatives manage to send over their weapons in the diplomatic pouch, but some embassies are squeamish about that kind of thing, and some operatives don't want to be associated with their embassies if they are in deep cover. Bert, who had been quietly asked to leave the Special Boat Service after kicking his way into a Taliban safe house in Pakistan and executing the six men inside, had set up a small business in Antequera. He had had to leave the service because the British Army cannot be seen to be engaged in illegal executions, especially in Muslim countries, but he had become a legend in the world of Special Ops and several songs had been written about him, all of which had to be sung drunk and involved colorful language of few syllables.

I had told him, in our own, particular jargon, that I did not want a Glock—a Google Lock—but my personal choice of sidearm, what he called a Sam Smith. Sam Smith was his choice of English bitter and shared its initials with Sig Sauer. Double and half again was the 226, following some obscure arithmetical logic of his own.

So that evening I would go and collect a gun.

THIRTEEN

I didn't take the A-45, the highway that ran from Malaga to Cordoba, and ultimately Madrid. That would have got me to Antequera in about an hour. Instead I took the wending A-357 as far as Pizarra, a town curiously named "Blackboard," and then the rustic A-7077 that wound and twisted through the hills and woods to the town of Alora, which sat nestled high on a mountain, like a white skirt around its castle. There I was stopped at a roadblock and asked to show my papers. The lieutenant who examined them searched my face with hostile eyes.

"Where are you going?"

I was going to tell him it was none of his goddamn business. Instead I smiled without feeling and told him, "Anterquera."

"Why? Why you go to Antequera?"

"Because that's where I kissed my first girlfriend and it has sentimental meaning for me. Why don't you ask my good friend Manuel Torreras Carbonell and demand he explain it to you?" He stared at me like he wanted to shoot me. It happens to some young men when you give them a uniform. I held his eye for a count of three and asked him, "Was there anything else, Lieutenant?"

He handed back my papers. As I took them I asked him, "What's your name?"

"Lieutenant Francisco Ballesteros."

I nodded. "I'll be sure to tell Manuel you were real polite and helpful."

He snapped the order to let me through the block and I wound my way through a village that was probably depressing in peacetime and now looked about as much fun as Sweden on the first Monday in January.

After that the road got really remote. The landscape was wild and startling, with valleys and plains broken up by sudden, steep mountains of gray rock that jutted out of the arid olive groves like the blackened teeth of long-dead giants.

By the time I arrived the blue sky was turning to a grainy dusk that was shrouding the city in lamplit gloom. Antequera is one of the most ancient cities in Spain, which is to say one of the most ancient in the world. When the Romans arrived, two hundred and twenty years before Christ, they already considered Antequera ancient and called it Antiquaria, which more or less translates as "the ancient one." Now, as I parked the Mustang and set off on foot among its maze of narrow, cobbled streets, I could feel that primeval age seeping from the churches, the plazas and the crooked houses, lit by old, iron lamps bolted to their sandstone walls.

It was a five-minute walk through the dusk into the evening, and when I arrived night had fallen and the cobbled square with its sandstone fountain in the middle was held in a pool of lamplight around which the shadows of houses and trees crowded and clustered. I crossed the square to the door, where two men, who had probably been old when the Romans arrived two thousand years back, sat at a table in the light of the open window under a faded Coca-Cola sign.

I pushed through the door into the warm noise and bustle of the bar, and went to the bar without looking to see if Bert was there. I knew he was. The barman jerked his chin at me and I told him, "*Cerveza, por favor.*"

He started to list all the beers he had so I pointed to the tap. When I had my beer I looked around and saw Bert sitting in the corner reading a book by Chris Ryan. I didn't see anyone who immediately stuck out as not being a habitual patron, so I crossed the floor and stood over him.

"Didn't we meet in Hawaii in '62?"

He frowned but didn't look up till he'd finished the paragraph. Then he squinted at me like I was hard to fathom.

"See, you think you're funny. But you're not."

"Thanks." I pulled out a chair and sat, and pointed to the book. "They criticize him for fabrication and not telling the true story, but then if he tried to tell the truth they'd criticize him for that too."

"Yeah. That's why I never wrote a book. If I did, all them pink, spineless wankers in Whitehall and DC would be out of a job. You've got six blokes raping and murdering innocent farmers and their families, who are just trying to make a decent fah—sorry, I forgot you was sensitive—trying to make a decent bleedin' living out of an unforgiving desert, and some geezer like me gets up one day and decides he has seen one too many dead child, one too many raped woman, one too many castrated, humiliated dad. And he goes, and he find the bastards what done it and he saves the taxpayer a trial by shooting them." He leaned forward and pointed a finger at my chest. "Now, I am willing to bet you ten grand, right here, right now, that there is not a person from Sydney to Calgary, by way of New York, Dublin and London, who would not applaud what that bloke did, once they had heard what those six other bastards had done first. Especially if they saw the photographs."

"You're probably right."

"I know I'm bleedin' right. Even your pink-lipped liberals would get it once they saw what them bastards did. But the powers that be don't want that. That ain't the name of the game. Divide, divide and conquer. *Divide et vince.* So who you gonna pop, then?"

"I could tell you, but then you'd have to kill me."

He grinned. "Modest. I know you're a dangerous bastard. I don't care who you take out. They're all as bloody corrupt as each other. That Musa's the worst. Not satisfied exploiting the oil, he wants to cozy up with the ragheads and turn Andalusia into an Islamic state. Like it used to be, he says."

"You talking to anyone? Anything I should know?"

He shook his head, "No, mate. I don't do that no more. Keep my nose clean. I have the sword of Damocles hanging over me. One foot wrong and I'm for the chopper."

As he said it the sound of the TV rose suddenly and the buzz of conversation died away. I saw Bert's eyes travel over my shoulder to the screen and I turned to look. Alvaro Romero was standing outside the Moncloa Palace. It was evening so I figured it was a live broadcast. He was speaking to a cluster of microphones. My Spanish was not good enough to follow what he was saying, but by the set of his jaw, and the cold glint in his eye, I didn't get the feeling he was talking about dialogue and compromise.

One guy slammed his hand on the bar and stalked out, leaving his wine half empty. Others looked away from the screen muttering. They didn't know whether to be mad or scared. I glanced at Bert. "What's he saying?"

Bert gave his head a single shake. A moment later the TV cut back to the new anchor and the bar erupted in angry voices. Bert said:

"He's given Musa a three-day deadline."

"A deadline for what and what are the consequences?"

"Full capitulation and Andalusia returns unconditionally to the Spanish crown, or all-out war."

"Three days, is that seventy-two hours or just sometime the day after the day after tomorrow?"

"Seventy-two hours. If you're going to do something, you'd better do it fast."

We had a couple more beers and some tapas, he gave me a newspaper and I made my way back to the parking lot where I'd left the Mustang. On the way, two armed soldiers stepped out of the inky shadows of a church, into the amber light of a lamp and pointed their rifles at me, rattling something at me in Spanish. I raised my hands and said, "*Americano, amigo Ministro Manuel Torreras Carbonell.*"

The guns wavered and one of them said, "Papers."

I showed him, they saluted and walked away. They have a saying in Spain, if you've got a godfather, you get to go to the christening. Apparently I had a godfather, but I wondered for how long. There was a growing tension in the air that was hard to ignore, and if the tanks started rolling in seventy-two hours, any Americans this side of the border would be very much *persona non grata*, fast tracked to some deep dungeon, probably out in the caves of Gore.

I climbed into the Mustang, slammed the door and followed the beams of my headlamps into the impenetrable darkness of the wilderness between Antequera and Malaga, where the mountains rose sudden and startling, like black behemoths against translucent night sky.

That was when the burner I had for Nero rang. I pressed the green button.

"Hey Mom."

"I have been hearing chatter and gossip."

"Are we very surprised?"

I followed the cones of amber light around a hairpin bend surrounded by blackness, listening to his silence, like he was wondering whether he was surprised. Finally he said, "Not really. More disappointed. It is hurtful when close friends gossip."

"You getting sensitive on me, Mom?"

"I cannot afford that luxury."

"That's what I thought. Listen, I'm driving right now. I'll call you later."

"I could use some good news. Find out what you can, but don't get bogged down. That is not your primary objective."

"I'll see to it. I'll call you later."

"Good."

I made it back to the hotel by nine PM and went straight to reception. There I asked the guy behind the desk if

Captain Aila Gallin was in her room. He checked and said she was. I took the phone from him and spoke loudly.

"Hey beautiful, you want to have dinner with me and Mitch York? I'll introduce you. We'll have some drinks. Dinner's on me. You can thank me later."

She was silent for a moment, then, "OK, anything I need to know?"

"Just get down here pronto. I miss you."

"I'm on my way."

I handed the phone to the receptionist and said, "Get me Mitch York, will you?"

It rang a couple of times and he said, "Mr. York, I have Mr. Mason here, he would like to speak with you."

He handed me the phone. "Mr. York, forgive me if it's a little late for us Yankees, but here the evening is just starting. I wonder if you would join me and Captain Gallin for dinner. She is particularly keen to meet you."

"I gather you have some news?"

I laughed. "Captain Gallin is always very entertaining, and exceptionally beautiful! But I think I might be able to make a contribution to the conversation as well."

"I'll be there."

"Say half an hour? We'll have cocktails at the table while we order."

"Sounds fine."

I hung up as Gallin emerged from the elevator and came toward me. She was in a long, royal blue dress with an immoral décolletage and an outrageous slash up her right leg. To make matters worse she had a string of diamonds around her throat that made you want to bite her neck. I figured if I wanted to draw attention, which I did, that was probably what I should do. So I walked toward her, took her in my arms and bit her shoulder. I had the pleasure, when I grinned at her afterwards, of seeing her cheeks flush.

"My goodness," she said, "you'd better cut back on your vitamins."

"Let's go to the bar and have a drink."

We crossed the lobby into the bar laughing noisily. There were maybe a dozen people there, mostly drunk journalists. Gallin sat on a stool. I put my arm round her waist and told the barman in a loud voice, "I am going to need a bottle of Dom Pérignon, very cold on ice."

Gallin laughed and leaned her head on my shoulder. The barman asked, "Dom Pérignon?"

"Yeah, and tell me where the bathroom is." I planted a kiss on Gallin's neck and asked her, "You go anywhere nice today, honey?"

"I *did*. It was a day of fascinating encounters. I'll tell you all about it when we're alone, bunny-wunny."

"I can't wait. I'll be right back, honey."

I walked out to the lobby, made sure nobody was looking at me and sprinted up the stairs. When I reached York's room I tapped on the door. After a moment it was opened by one of his two gorillas. He frowned at me.

I said, "I have a confidential message for Mitch from Nero."

He stepped back to let me in and closed the door behind me. There are certain blows which I practice over and over. They are the simple, decisive and above all silent ones. This one is delivered with the web between your thumb and your index finger, which is drawn taut when your thumb is extended. It must be delivered very hard and very fast to the trachea, and that was what I did as he closed the door.

It silenced him, because he couldn't breathe, but it didn't kill him. I did that when I stamped on the back of his neck. His feet twitched and jerked a few times, but otherwise he died in silence.

I straightened my jacket and walked smiling into the living room section of the suite. The other gorilla was there holding a magazine, echoing his dead pal's frown. I said, Where's Mitch? I need to talk to him?"

"He's in the bedroom. Where's...?" He was frowning harder, trying to look past me into the hall.

"He's gone," I said and pulled the P226 from my waistband and shot him between the eyes. When I had told Bert I wanted a *quiet* Sam Smith, he had understood I needed to make a quiet kill, and he had fitted the P226 with an MODX-9 titanium, segmented suppressor. Because it comes in segments, you can make the suppressor longer or shorter. Shorter is louder, but it fits more comfortably in your waistband.

I heard York shouting from the bedroom, "Who the hell is that?"

I pushed through the door and smiled at him. He had on his shirt and his socks. I smiled.

"Seems I caught you with your pants down, Mitch."

"What the hell...?"

"There's been chatter." His face went gray. I added, "Gossip. See, there were no Russian fighter-bombers in Baza. Only three people on the planet had that information, Mitch, Nero, me and you. And you were the only one who believed it was true."

"I don't know what you're talking about."

"There has been gossip on the airwaves, Mitch. Don't make this harder than it needs to be. You know we do that better than anybody. We should be the Five Ears instead of the Five Eyes, right? Just a couple of hours after I fed you the intel, they were chattering about it, that you had been fed false intelligence, that your cover had been blown. You're a dead man walking, Mitch. If we don't take you down, they will."

"Go to hell! I have friends…"

But even as he was saying it he knew it was no longer true. He knew the herd abandoned the sick and the injured to be eaten by the wolves. I leaned on the doorjamb.

"This is real simple. You come back in for debriefing. You tell me who your contacts were in Russia, who you worked for. The alternative is, I throw you off the balcony."

For a moment there was defiance in his eyes. "I'd like to see you try!"

I smiled. "I might have to blow your kneecap off first, but I'm happy to do that. Who were you working for in Russia, Mitch?"

He faltered for just a second, then rallied. "Screw you! You can't do this to me. You know how much weight I carry in DC? I'm untouchable! I'll sink you *and* Nero!"

"I'm running out of time. Do I need to spell it out? You have three options: come in and be debriefed, go to prison for the rest of your life, or get killed here in your room by a presumed burglar. I have to tell you, I don't much care for people who betray their country, so you are playing a dangerous game right now, and the clock is ticking. What's it going to be?"

FOURTEEN

He came at me like a bull. He knew he was going down, but he wasn't going easy. It was a shame. He had information that would have been invaluable to ODIN, about who he was reporting to in Russia, and perhaps even people we could lean on to persuade Russia and Iran to back away from the Spanish conflict. Sometimes it just takes one man to falter for a major conflict to deflate. It would have been a nice solution, but it was not to be. Mitch York was not the kind of man to falter for long, and he had done all his faltering with me.

He roared and charged, with his flapping shirt, his naked legs and his socks. I delivered a thundering right hook to his head which, partly due to the Sig Sauer I was holding, turned his legs to Jell-O. As he staggered to his knees I grabbed his collar and dragged him to the open balcony. There I shoved half his body over the rail and told him, "Your choice, Mitch. You come home and talk to Nero, or you talk to the sidewalk."

His voice came as a rasp. "Screw you, Mason. She'll get you. There is nothing you can do to stop her. She'll find you and she'll find Nero, and she will destroy—"

I didn't see much point in waiting to hear the rest. I grabbed his shorts and tipped him over.

I was already inside by the time he hit the ground. It's not the kind of sound you hang around to listen to, somewhere between a thud and a crunch; and it's not something you would choose to do to a fellow human being, either. But betraying your country and sending a nation into an unnecessary war, where innocent lives are placed in the firing line, is a crime that, in my book, is paid in blood. I wiped my prints off the Sig, squeezed it into one of the gorilla's hands and left a confusing mess for the Andalusian cops to try and unravel.

I took the stairs three at a time and by the time I reached the lobby those people who were not outside on the sidewalk were staring out the door or the plate-glass windows. They all had their backs to me. I slipped into the bar unseen and Gallin and I emerged a moment later to see what all the fuss was about.

The barman and the receptionist came in from outside. The receptionist was talking rapidly on his cell. The barman approached us. He was shaking his head.

"*Señor* York, he is..." He spread his hands, hunched his shoulders, turned and gestured with both hands toward where he imagined *Señor* York's balcony to be. "He is *fall*..."

Gallin said, "He *fell*?"

"From his balcony, on the sidewalk!"

"Is hew badly hurt? We were going to dine with him."

The poor guy started to weep. "If he is alive, it, it...," he shook his head, "God forgive me, if he is alive, it is worse, he is all broken. He cannot live. Police is comin' now."

We went back into the bar to our table to drink very cold Dom Perignon and wait for the cops. Gallin crossed her legs and sipped and told me, "You're a son of a bitch, Mason."

"Those are the very same words my mother uttered when she handed me over to the orphanage. It was a hard day for me. She didn't even let me keep Fluffems."

"You said you were going to introduce me. We had questions for Mitch York."

"Yeah, well, needs must when the devil drives, honeybunny. He'd answered my most important question, and he didn't seem real willing to talk anymore. By the way, while we're on the subject, how does the Mossad deal with traitors?"

She shrugged and looked away. "You mean after the period of reflection and social readjustment in meaningful dialogue with their rabbi, in which they explore the childhood issues that made them question their roots and give them a sense of not belonging?"

"Yeah, after that period."

"We shoot them."

"That's what I thought. Are you going to tell me where he went today?"

I refilled our glasses while she thought about it, and added, "Let's not kid ourselves, Gallin. If Iran gets a foothold in Europe, in an Islamic Andalusia, we are all losers, but the biggest loser is Israel. Putting it bluntly, if you use a tactical nuke on Iran, you don't care much what the impact is on her neighbors—Iraq, Kuwait, Syria, Turkey—"

She frowned at me, irritated. "Of course we care, Mason,"

"OK, we all care, but let's face it, these are countries that are no friends of Israel. But here, in Spain? You can't use a tactical nuke in Spain because her neighbors are Portugal, France and Italy. We all lose if Andalusia becomes a satellite of Iran and Russia, but nobody loses more than Israel. Agreed?"

"Of course." She said it quietly, with a hint of resentment.

"So share with me Gallin, who did he go and see?"

She looked me straight in the eye. "You going to tell me why you threw him off his balcony?"

"You know I will."

She gave her chin a small jerk toward the entrance to the bar behind my shoulder. I turned and looked. There were two cops in blue uniforms and one guy in his late fifties with gray hair and a suit he'd inherited from his dad. He was talking to the uniforms. They nodded and he walked over to where we were sitting. I stood as he arrived and offered my hand. He scrutinized me with dark eyes before shaking.

"I am Inspector of Police David Garcia. You are Mr. Alex Mason?"

"Yes, and this is Captain Aila Gallin."

He looked at her, nodded once and turned back to me. "You were associated with Mr. York?"

I gestured to a chair and we sat.

"I represent a consortium of oil investors in the United States, Inspector. Your minister for oil, Manuel Torreras, had asked me to invite one of my principals from the consortium to come, so that he could meet him. Mr. York offered to come. He arrived just this morning and we were due to dine tonight." I shrugged and shook my head, looking at Gallin. "When I spoke to him on the phone at reception he seemed perfectly sober..."

Garcia frowned. "Why do you say this?"

I gestured toward the bar. "The barman said he had fallen from his balcony. I assumed he had been drinking..." I trailed off, wondering whether I had overplayed my hand.

Garcia shook his head. "You will be staying in Malaga a few more days?"

"I think so. I imagine I'll have another meeting with Mr. Torreras to see where we go from here."

He hesitated, then spoke quietly. "The Spanish Navy is going to blockade the ports of Huelva, Cadiz, Algeciras, Malaga, Almeria and Motril. The Spanish air force has made an exclusion zone over Andalusia. My advice to you," he glanced at Gallin, "to you both, is drive tonight to Gibraltar." He stood. "You are lucky. You have somewhere to run to. We must stay and take the punishment." He nodded to us both and left, poking a cigarette in his mouth as he went.

Gallin sipped her champagne and watched me. "We are running out of time."

I glanced at my watch. "A little over sixty-seven hours."

She shook her head. "Less. Remember half the Spanish navy is under Andalusian control in Rota and Cartagena. My guess? What's left will move to blockade the ports in the next few hours," she paused and smiled, "its first significant action in a hundred and twenty years, since the Americans sank their entire fleet in 1898."

"Your point being that their navy is not very experienced?"

"Something like that. Historically they are pretty good at losing all their ships through acts of incompetence that are hard to understand."

I was frowning, scratching my chin and trying to see where she was going. "It doesn't take a lot of skill or experience to blockade a port, Gallin."

Now she was looking smug. "True. On the other hand, traditionally, Shia and Sunni Muslims hate each other almost as much as they hate each other. However, there are some notable exceptions."

"OK..."

"Iran, mainly Shia, for example, has extremely close and deepening ties with Algeria. Another country which has very close ties with Algeria, going all the way back to its socialist past—"

"Is Russia."

"Bingo. Our intelligence and my gut tells me that as what is left of the Spanish fleet steams in from Menorca and Mallorca, they are going to encounter resistance in the form of maritime guerrilla warfare from paramilitary volunteers out of Algeria and possibly even Morocco, giving the Andalusian ships in Cartagena the chance, if they choose to take it, to sail out and finish them off." She gave a short, dry laugh. "The Russians and the Iranians are not going to get stymied that easily. While your Western politicians are wringing their hands and pissing in their knickers, the Russians are developing strategies. And as for the Spanish, the only wars they've won in the last five hundred years have been against themselves." She thrust out her lower lip and gave her head a single shake. "The sinking of the Spanish fleet will make it very hard for the NATO allies to remain neutral. It will put an Islamic, fundamentalist nation on the UK's doorstep, beside Gibraltar, controlling access to the Mediterranean. What's next? An Islamic Andalusia reclaiming Gib? They'll have to act."

"So all hell is going to break out in—"

"Sometime between the next ten minutes and the next sixty hours."

"Narrowing it down, we have between six and forty-eight hours."

"Maybe."

I pulled my cell from my pocket and called Nero. It rang once.

"Are you using an untraceable telephone?"

"Hey Mom! You know me! All about doing the right thing."

"Report."

"OK, so I'm sitting here with Aila, and she says hi. Uncle Mikey couldn't make it. He's having his teeth extracted."

"What?"

"From the sidewalk. But Aila tells me she went with him this morning and he had some great encounters, and she's going to tell me all about them."

"Good. I have spoken to Gabriel in London. Cooperate with her."

"I plan to, Mommy dear. But we may have to leave soon. It sounds like the Spanish navy plan to blockade the ports, and, I don't know how to tell you this but Aila thinks our neighbors might..." I searched for some way to say it that would not involve too many buzzwords or attract the attention of the journalists who were drifting back into the bar. "They might want to lend a hand."

"You mean Algeria might lend Andalusia a hand on behalf of Iran. I should have thought that was obvious. Personally I give you less than forty-eight hours to do something useful. Find out to whom he was reporting, and Alex, inform Mr. Torreras Carbonell that I shall be coming to see him within the next few hours."

"That is a really, really bad idea, sir."

"Anything else?"

"Yeah, just before he tried to eat the sidewalk, Uncle Mikey told me not to worry."

"Not to worry about what?"

"Aunty would find us." I laughed. "He said she was unstoppable."

"A woman."

"He said, 'She—'"

"I'll be in touch. I do not need collecting at the airport. Find out whom he was talking to."

"Bye Mom. Love you too." But I was talking to a dead line. I sighed at Gallin. "He says he's coming."

"That's stupid."

"I agree."

"It's..." She shrugged and shook her head the way Mediterraneans do. "It's like a brain going to a boxing match and leaving its fists at home."

"That is a really weird simile, Gallin."

"Yeah." She nodded. "But accurate."

I guessed it was. I sighed and sipped my champagne. "It's a pretty formidable brain," I said. "I guess he knows what he's doing."

"I sure hope so."

"I have to admit, though, it's a pretty weird thing to do. What does he think he can achieve by coming here?"

"Hmm..." It was a sound of uncertain agreement. Then she added, "And why does he want you to inform Torreras? Surely he must be able to contact him direct."

"You'd think." I thought a moment and set down my glass. "He's a genius. I am not. And if that's what he wants, that's what I had better do."

I called Torreras.

"Mr. Mason, what a great pleasure to speak to you again. I hope you enjoyed your visit to Baza."

"It was fascinating, thank you. Listen, we've had something of a tragedy here. I don't know if you have been informed yet, but Mitch York, our representative who just arrived here today, has had a fatal accident."

I waited. There was a long silence at the other end, followed by, "A fatal accident?"

"Yeah. It's quite bizarre. He seems to have fallen from his balcony while we were waiting for him to dine with us. It's really very tragic."

"Yes, indeed."

"However, I have spoken to the head of our consortium, Mr. Nero, and he will be coming over personally to talk to you. He is really motivated. He asked me to let you know he's coming, though I am sure he'll be in touch himself before long."

He thanked me and hung up with a quiet, thoughtful air to his voice. I shrugged and smiled at Gallin.

"Come on, let's go and have dinner. Maybe they'll have a pianist to play 'As Time Goes By' for us."

She smiled and arched an eyebrow at me. Will we always have Malaga?"

I held out my hand to her. "Always, but I warn you, I am not going to send you off in a plane with some peace campaigner. These days they wear hoodies and smash windows."

She squeezed my arm as we made for the dining room. "Are you going to keep me all to yourself?"

"Every little bit of you," I told her.

FIFTEEN

Colonel Alexandrina Vitsin twisted her thin lips into something that should have been a smile, but wasn't. It was a complicated expression made of resentment and hatred leavened by satisfaction. The satisfaction came largely from the memory of making the whore weep. She had come into the office smug and cocky. "I have made many officers smile," she had said, "even generals. I am sure I can make you smile too."

She had been right about that, at least. She had made her smile, but at the cost of her own tears. She'd be sitting on soft cushions for the next couple of weeks, that was for sure. Colonel Vitsin barked a hard, cruel laugh into the silence of her dark office as she remembered the raw, pink cheeks. The girl had been limping and sobbing when she paid her.

"You will remember me," Vitsin had told her as she handed over the cash. "No man, no general, ever made such an impression on you, or paid you so well. Am I right?"

The girl had nodded. "Yes."

"Yes what?"

"Yes, Mistress."

She had glimpsed the dark side, she had not liked it and she had fled. That was what Alexandrina Vitsin liked. She liked when they were young and fresh, she liked when the saw the darkness approaching and panicked, and she liked when they fled. Then she gave them money, lots of money, to help them flee. She was intelligent enough to know that she was projecting, trying to save her own soul by proxy, and she also knew that her own soul was beyond salvation. But when she saw them, young and blonde, with flushed pink cheeks, wet with tears, hurrying away clutching their money, swearing secretly that they would never return, for a moment, just for a moment, she felt something like peace, a hiatus in her habitual hatred of all humans.

As the image of the raw, pink buttocks faded from her memory, she bent her mind instead to the telephone call she had just received from Dr. Elena Montijano, professor of English philology at the University of Malaga.

"He told me he could not call you. He told me he was afraid they suspected him. He told me about a man they call Nero."

That had made the colonel sit up and pay attention. Nero, the name that had come to her from here and from there, that seemed to filter through from some suspected agency beneath and beyond the Central Intelligence Agency; an agency that lurked in the shadows.

"Nero? What did he tell you about Nero?"

"He said that Nero had a special department within the CIA. Nobody knew exactly what the department did, but it was somehow connected with the NSA."

This much Colonel Vitsin knew or suspected already. Montijano went on.

"He said he feared that Nero had sent him here to Spain as a trap, and so he was afraid to communicate directly with you."

"What made him think this?"

"There was an agent whom he believed was from Central Intelligence who met him from the airport. His name was Mason, Alex Mason. He told him he had seen Iranian fighter-bombers in Baza, beside the oil wells. But when he informed the Minister for Oil that they had been seen—"

Vitsin's voice was like a rasp. "There are no Iranian fighter-bombers in Baza!"

"No, Colonel, that's correct, but when the minister heard this he made phone calls, and it was established that there were no Iranian war planes in Baza. And this made Mr. York think that he had been suspected and tested. I don't really understand..."

The woman trailed off. Nero had suspected Mitch. Mitch had always been a big mouth and now he had blown his cover. Nero had smelt the rat and sent him to Spain where he had fed him false information through Mason, information only Nero, Mason and Mitch would have; and from GCHQ's listening post in Gibraltar they had monitored the airwaves for references to the nonexistent fighter-bombers in Baza. Once they'd intercepted those references, they would have known that Mitch York was the Kremlin's man. He would now either be turned, or, more likely, he would slip on a banana skin and fall backward onto a salad fork.

Colonel Vitsin had read this once in a book by the Harvard Lampoon. It had been four weeks before she had realized it was a humorous allusion to assassination.

Montijano's voice chattered on. "So, what he really wanted was for me to tell you he had to go off the air for a while and that his cover had been compromised."

She had hung up. The loss of Mitch York at this stage was not important. He had served his purpose. What had really put her in the mood to celebrate had been the panicky call from Torreras, the fat, bald, stupid Minister for Oil. She reached out a hand for her cigarettes, shook one free and poked it in her mouth straight from the packet. She lit it from a purple disposable lighter which she clutched in her fist like the hilt of a dagger. She breathed in the smoke, taking it deep into her lungs through an open mouth and held it there, as though it were the smoke from marijuana.

"We have a man here called Mason. He says he wants to buy Andalusian oil. I told him we want to meet his principal, like you said, but his principal, Mitch York, comes to me and tells me that Mason has seen SU-22 Russian fighter-bombers in Baza. But there are no SU-22 Russian fighter-bombers in Baza!"

"Stop panicking, Mr. Torreras."

"I called the Minister for Defense and I called the president, Mr. Musa, and I asked them, what the hell? They both told me, 'There are no Iranian fighter-bombers in Baza!'"

She had closed her eyes, sighed and shaken her head. "What happened next, Mr. Torreras?"

"Then I am informed by the police that Mr. York has been murdered, with his two bodyguards. It looks maybe like one of the bodyguards killed him, but it is not clear."

"Don't worry about this. It was almost certainly Mr. Mason who killed him. You must arrest him and execute him."

"What about the Israeli woman who is with him, Captain Gallin?"

"Kill her too."

"And Mr. Nero?"

"What?"

"Mr. Nero, the head of the consortium, he is coming personally to talk with me. He will be here tomorrow."

She had grinned broadly with ugly black and yellow teeth. She had watched her right hand tremble where it rested on her desk. A hot flush of excitement had burned in her belly.

"Arrest him as he comes off the plane. I will be there. Hold him until I arrive."

She had hung up and sat for a moment unable to control her excitement. She had crushed the cigarette and taken another with trembling hands. Then she had called her secretary. "Elena, arrange a flight for me to Malaga, tonight, as soon as possible. And Elena, while I wait, get me another girl. Young. I want to celebrate."

SIXTEEN

WE HAD DINED, THOUGH FROM A MENU WHICH THE head waiter informed us was greatly reduced. We had turbot and salmon mousse—not mixed together, but a portion of each on a plate with a béchamel sauce, which we spread on dry crackers. We accompanied this with a bottle of Ana de Codorniu, very cold in frosted glasses, and followed it with a leg of suckling lamb broiled in honey and eucalyptus, and a bottle of *Muga Gran Reserva* from 2021.

We didn't talk much. The food and the wine were too good to talk, and we both had a background awareness that this might be our last supper; and unless we could come up with something truly memorable, like, "This is my body you eat," it was best to observe a respectful silence.

Over cheese and crackers, espresso coffee and a generous glass of twenty-one-year-old Bushmills, I said, "They'll arrest him."

She nodded assent while she chewed, then asked, "What for?"

"Because the Russians want him. They'll accuse him of spying, arrest him and send him to Moscow."

"Is this based on analysis or just a gut feeling?"

"It's a gut feeling with its roots in experience. The Russians have known there was an agency in the shadows behind the CIA for a long time, and for a long time they have been trying to get a bead on the director. York didn't know much, but he knew enough to focus Moscow's sights on Nero."

"So why the hell is he coming? Either he's lost it or he is playing a very deep game."

I sipped and savored. "Knowing Nero it's probably both."

She winced, like she wanted to be amused but it was too serious for that. "They'll torture him and kill him."

"He's too smart to let that happen."

"Very smart people also go very crazy. The question is, what are we going to do if they arrest him?"

I shook my head. "Not a lot, because if they arrest him off the plane, which they probably will, they will either be in the process of arresting us at the same time, or already have arrested us."

She grunted. It was an oddly pretty sound coming from her. "So what...?" She shrugged, narrowed her eyes and shook her head all at the same time, like the world was too stupid to be understood. "He's coming here for the purpose of getting arrested? Even if you're a genius, what's the point in that?"

I sliced the last piece of cheese in half, put each half on a cracker and handed her one. "I don't know. Let's think it through. Either they'll arrest him at the airport, or they'll take him to some official building to talk to him before arresting him. The chances are Torreras will want the glory of having captured and interrogated him, so they'll probably keep him in Malaga."

She was nodding as she chewed and pointed at me as she swallowed. "And you and I will be the aces up his sleeve. They will come for us before they arrest him off the plane, they will separate us, torture and interrogate us and play us against each other."

I nodded. "They will have two objectives. One, to find out how NATO plans to respond to the war in Spain, and two, to penetrate ODIN on behalf of the Russians. We need to be making a move, and you need to change into something more comfortable."

"We need a plan."

I stood and pulled her to her feet. "We'll develop it in the car. Right now we must practice some misdirection."

I put my arm around her and led her to reception. There I squeezed her to me while she giggled, and told the receptionist, "If anybody comes for me, I am not in my room, understood?"

I slipped him a hundred bucks and led Gallin to the elevator where I gave her a long, lingering kiss while the elevator descended from the top floor. The doors pinged and slid open and we stepped inside, where she thumped me hard on the chest.

"There are laws against that, pal."

"There should be," I told her. "That was way too nice."

"Charm will get you nowhere."

The doors slid open again.

She unlocked her door and as I closed it she was stripping off her dress. I tried to focus on a plan while she pulled on a pair of jeans over what was really just the ghost of a pair of violet panties. Then there was a pair of brown leather military style boots, a T-shirt with a picture of Bruce Lee on it, a shoulder holster with a Sig P226 and finally she shrugged on a brown leather jacket as she turned to face me.

I made the face of indecision. "I don't know, honey. I think the dress, really."

"This is not the time. Not if you want to keep your cojones."

I nodded. "Down to the parking garage and out on foot. Then steal a car."

"Go!"

In the elevator on the way down, she said, "And once we have the car?"

I didn't answer.

The elevator came to a halt, the doors opened and we stepped out into the gloom and grime of the subterranean parking garage. We crossed through the half-light, past the darkened, sleeping cars and climbed the ramp out into the street. It was a weird sight. I had been to Malaga city on many occasions. It was a city of light, crowded streets, bustling restaurants, cafés and bars. Now the amber street-lamps shone on empty sidewalks and cast dark, empty shadows. From where we stood we saw a police car slide past at the end of the road.

"The curfew is going to make this difficult. My pass from Manuel Torreras won't do us much good if there's a warrant out for my arrest."

She sighed and ran her fingers through her hair. "Hell

Mason, it would help if we had a plan. But we don't even have an *objective*, let alone a plan. What are we doing?"

"Our objective right now is to avoid detection and arrest long enough so that we can decide on an objective and make a plan."

She examined my face a moment with a strange mixture of affection and despair. "How have you survived this long, Mason?"

"I don't know. I think my great, great-grandmother was Irish."

She rolled her eyes. "Come on, and when I tell you, start singing softly, like you were amiably drunk." She headed off toward the Calle Larios, the main pedestrianized drag that runs through the center of Malaga. I followed.

"Amiably drunk? Are you serious? Where are we going?"

"Shut up."

She led me down a couple of narrow back streets. They were dark, silent and lonely. A third led, after thirty or forty yards, to an intersection where pallid, amber light bathed a pedestrianized street, which I guessed was the Calle Larios. She slipped under my right arm and put her left around my waist, and said, "Now—"

"What?"

"Now, start singing now."

I searched my memory banks and intoned, in a manly baritone, "In Dublin's fair city, where the girls are so pretty, I first set my eyes on sweet Molly Malone..."

We turned into the broad, empty street, with its huge window displays looking strangely manic and bizarre in that silent desolation. She pulled on me and pushed with her hip so that we staggered slightly. About thirty or forty yards away there was a Land Rover Defender parked across the road. Two young soldiers stood with rifles hung around their necks. They were staring at us, with the limpid light casting shadows across their faces. In an instant I knew we were going to die there, and I thought that, as ways of dying go, it was not the worst.

Gallin said, "Keep singing, asshole!"

"As she wheeled her wheelbarrow, through street broad and narrow, crying cockles, and mussels, alive, alive-oh..."

The irony was not lost on me as I sang, with my belly on fire, expecting death at any second. But Gallin led us, slightly unsteady, toward the soldiers, calling out in a very English accent, "*Hola, por favor, ayuda!*" Which means pretty much, "Hello, help please."

One of the little bastards put his rifle to his shoulder and trained it on us. The other snapped, "*Alto! Papeles!*" Then he added, half screaming, "*Mn'e rft w amd wjwd dard!*

No saben que hay toque de queda?" The last bit was Spanish and meant something like, "There's a curfew, for crying out loud." But there was something odd in his accent, and the bit in the middle sounded like Farsi to me. This guy was not Spanish.

Getting into my role, I sang, "Alive, alive-oh-ho, alive, alive-oh-ho, he ain't Spanish no-ho, crying cockles and mussels, alive, alive-oh..."

Gallin, dragged me closer, bumbling in Spanglish, "*Por favor, hotel, Puerto,* speak English? *Señor Manuel Torreras, amigo. El tener papeles.*"

I had to admit she was good and I felt a wave of admiration. First she showed we were not a threat: a couple of drunks with the woman in charge. Then she mentioned a government minister as a friend, and finally pointed to me and said I had the papers that proved it. She was good.

He waved us forward and spoke in English that was as bad as Gallin's Spanish. "Papers! Show me papers!"

We approached. I stopped singing and said, "*Viva Andalusia! Andalusia bueno!*"

He looked at me like he wanted to eat my liver, so I shut up and reached in my pocket for my papers. By then I'd seen the badge on his arm. He was a captain in the Iranian army. We were a couple of feet away and his pal, who had lowered his rifle, stepped up. He was an Iranian grunt. I handed over my papers, and as I did so Gallin said, in a flat, toneless voice, "You take the guy with the rifle."

A right hook is a punch you don't often see a woman deliver. I really wish I hadn't been so busy delivering a lethal right knuckle jab to the grunt's windpipe. As his eyes bulged and he started to turn purple, I spun him around and broke his neck with an arm lock. But I caught Gallin's right hook out of the corner of my eye.

It was lightning fast. She stepped forward and slightly to her right, twisted on the ball of her foot and *wham!* She drove her right fist straight through his jaw. For a moment his legs were like sound waves on an electronic screen, but before he could sink to the sidewalk she drove her left fist into his liver. That probably killed him, but for the sake of thoroughness she locked her elbow under his chin and twisted. Then she let him drop, grinned at me and offered me a high five. "Nice straight lead. Help me get them in the back."

We took their weapons, their shirts and their caps and bundled the bodies in the back of the Land Rover. Then I climbed behind the wheel and Gallin got in beside me. We glanced at each other and she asked, "So what's the plan?"

I frowned and nodded. "I have absolutely no idea."

"We need to dump the bodies and get to Nero before they do!"

I shook my head. "No—"

"*What?*"

"Nero is the smartest guy I have ever met. He has an IQ up in the hundred-and-sixties. If he has come here it's for a reason, and if we try to snatch him at the airport, not only will we get ourselves and him killed, he will be really mad."

"Nero dead *and* mad would be something to see."

"He has a plan. I have never known Nero do something stupid. Crazy, yes, but stupid never. We wait outside the airport and when they pick him up we follow, we see where they take him and..."

I trailed off and she said, "We take it from there."

"It's about all we can do."

I fired up the engine and we pulled away slowly, down toward the port. Gallin said:

"You know there is an officer in charge of overseeing these blocks and sentry posts. They will recognize the Land Rover and stop us."

"That is almost certainly correct."

I pulled onto the main drag along the port. It was completely empty. I turned right toward the freeway and the airport. Gallin said: "So what do we do if that happens."

"Shoot them and take their vehicle."

She nodded and seemed to relax. "That's a good plan."

SEVENTEEN

THE SLEEK, WHITE GULFSTREAM TOUCHED DOWN
on the tarmac at four AM. The roar of the two powerful
engines switched to a scream that echoed across the empty
runways as the airbrakes kicked in. The jet, registered as AF
32/5, taxied through the dawn, among the whine of its
turbines, and came to rest outside Terminal Two, where four
Guardia Civil Range Rovers stood waiting around a dark
blue Audi A8. A bald man in an ill-fitting suit waited
outside the Audi, and beside him a captain of the Guardia
Civil, and a colonel.

The whine of the turbines died away and a moment later
the door of the plane opened and a giant appeared silhou-
etted against the glow of the cabin. As he descended the
steps the four men approached and waited, and as Nero's
foot touched the black asphalt the two soldiers saluted
crisply and Manuel Torreras held out his hand.

"Mr. Nero, it is a great honor to welcome you to the
Andalusian Republic on behalf of the Andalusian people. I

am Manuel Torreras, the Minister for Oil, this is Colonel Matias Pratt and Captain Vicente Garcia. Our president, Don Benjamin Musa, is very anxious to welcome you at the Palace of San Telmo in Seville, but first I am sure you would like a comfortable bed and a few hours' sleep."

Nero listened, immobile, then nodded. "I would indeed. Four hours should suffice. I believe my associate, Mr. Mason is at the Marriott in Malaga."

Mr. Torreras smiled and gestured toward the limousine. "Please, we are anxious to make your stay as comfortable as possible."

Nero followed Torreras the short distance across the tarmac to the waiting Audi. A soldier opened the door for him and Torreras climbed in on the far side. The captain and the colonel got in the rear of the lead Range Rover and the three vehicles moved in convoy out of the airport compound. Once on the road, as the horizon over the sea began to turn a pale blue-gray, the convoy picked up speed moving along the main artery that skirted the city. Nero watched without surprise as one turn off into the city after another slipped by. As the city began to fall behind them he turned to Torreras.

"Am I being kidnapped, Mr. Torreras?"

The man's shiny, round face broke into a shrill laugh. "My dear Mr. Nero, good heavens no! The president is not currently in Malaga, we are taking you to the castle of Almodóvar, the home of the Marquis of Motilla, Rafael de Solís Beaumont y Martínez. You will be extremely comfortable there and President Musa will come to meet you for luncheon."

Nero considered the man from under hooded eyes. "I

will be glad to see him," he said after a moment. "The president was keen that I should deliver a personal message to him."

"Of course." Torreras smiled and the lights of the passing streetlamps glinted on his bald head and the lenses of his spectacles. "You can convey your message from the president over what I believe you Americans call brunch." He chuckled. "Very funny, half breakfast, half lunch. Brunch."

"What is our ETA?"

"Shortly before six in the morning."

Nero closed his eyes and a few seconds later he was snoring softly.

They drove at speed along the empty freeway as the sun bled into the sky behind them. At just before five thirty, at Guadalcazar, just outside Cordoba, they turned west and followed the snaking Guadalquivir River to the foothills of the Sierra Morena. Here Nero opened his eyes and saw, through the windshield, the startling silhouette of the castle of Almodóvar, black against the red sky, perched on top of an almost perfectly conical hill around which the white village sprawled in the dawn.

Torreras saw him looking and smiled. "The castle is almost one and a half thousand years old. And before the castle there was a Roman fortress."

Nero arched an eyebrow at him. "It is older than that, Mr. Torreras. That hill is artificial and dates back at least to the Neolithic period. During the Bronze Age it was occupied by the Turdetani at the time of Tartessos. I wonder if the Marquis of Motilla realizes what treasures he has under his castle."

The crossed a narrow bridge over the Guadalquivir

River, then passed over the railway bridge and soon they were winding up the side of the conical mountain at the top of which the castle stood in stark silhouette against the crimson sky.

Behind and beneath them a military Land Rover pulled into the parking lot at the base of the hill.

The great doors of the castle swung open and the convoy of three vehicles drove into the courtyard. Ahead of them the colonel and the captain jumped down from the Range Rover, followed by two soldiers. Behind them four more soldiers spilled from the second Range Rover. The captain opened the door for Nero and saluted as he climbed out. Over the roof of the limo Nero gave Torreras a baleful look.

"Are all these soldiers a sign of Andalusia's courtesy toward a representative of the United States Government, Mr. Torreras?"

Torreras shrugged. "We are at war, Mr. Nero. We are anxious to protect you. Captain Garcia will show you to your suite. I recommend you rest. Anything you need, please let Captain Garcia know and he will provide it for you."

The captain led Nero into the ancient sandstone building, up a broad, winding staircase, past a galleried landing and finally to a suite of rooms in the west wing. The soldiers followed behind with his luggage.

He had a spacious bedroom with an ornate, ancient four-poster bed and an open fireplace, there was an en-suite bathroom with what seemed to be early Victorian plumbing, with gold fitments set in heavy marble, and a comfortable, if overly ornate sitting room with three arched, leaded windows that overlooked the vast sweep of the Guadalquivir valley, where it stretched away toward Seville, Cadiz and the Atlantic Ocean.

The soldiers deposited his bags and the captain clicked his heels like a German and bowed twenty-two-and-a-half degrees from the waist.

"Is there anything the *señor* wishes?"

Nero glanced at his watch. It was five minutes past six.

"Call me at ten. I shall want scrambled eggs, slightly underdone, on brown toast, fresh croissants, plenty of strong black coffee, butter, not margarine, and bitter marmalade."

"I shall see to it, *señor*. Sleep well."

The captain left. Nero heard the key in the lock. He was not surprised. He had expected it. He made his way to the bedroom, kicked off his shoes, stripped and lay down to sleep for three hours.

———

THREE HUNDRED YARDS away as the crow flies, if the crow happens to be in a steep nosedive, I sat next to Gallin and watched the sun bleed all over the horizon. In the imposing castle three hundred yards above us, I watched the few lights there were wink off as the dawn cleared away the shadows. Half a mile away to the south two young Iranian soldiers floated naked and dead in the Guadalquivir River, on their long journey to the sea.

I frowned at Gallin. "Gallin, why are you here?"

"What are you talking about?"

"This is not your mission. Why are you here. I mean, what *is* your mission?"

"Well, your dad talked to my dad, and—"

"Come on! Be serious."

She shrugged. "In as much as I can tell you anything, my job was to try and find out to what degree Iran was involved in this coup. But then Nero talked to Gabriel in London—"

"Your dad. Why do you call him Gabriel?"

"When it's work I call him Gabriel. He taught me that. Business is business. Anyway, I don't know what Nero told him, but he told me to seek you out and help you."

"Help me? I don't need help, Gallin. I mean, it's great you're here, but I don't *need* help."

"Right."

"I mean, I could help you. It doesn't have to be *you* helping *me...* 'Seek him out, Gallin, and use his help.'"

"Right. I get it."

"So we're here." I sighed and rubbed my face. "Nero's decision to come here has really complicated things. My mission was, like you, find out to what extent the Iranians are a part of this. Plus, who is driving this in Russia? If it gets too hot, get out. Cross over to Gibraltar, fly to London, debrief..."

I trailed off.

She nodded. "Nero's behavior is weird all right. It's like you said, he must know what he's doing. But it's hard to fathom." She turned to face me. "So what do we do? We know where he is. He's up there. What next? We haven't got a lot of time."

I thought about it, and as the sun inched up over the horizon I had a moment of something like clarity.

"He's counting on us behaving as we would, spontaneously, in a situation like this. So we have to do exactly what we would do."

She nodded, expressionlessly. "That's it? That's your plan? Your moment of clarity? Your vision? Do what we would do? That is the biggest crock of bullshit I have heard in my entire career."

"Listen, smartass. Communications were compromised by Mitch York until last night. My communication with Nero was *very* limited. So two gets you twenty he is relying on us to act intuitively. We've worked together a long time. We have a kind of rapport."

She curled her lip. "Well, if you put it like that. What does your intuition say?"

I shrugged. "You're the woman."

She looked up at the castle as the sun's first rays touched the sandstone walls. "One," she said, "we drive up and tell them we are part of Nero's negotiating team. We were supposed to meet him at the airport, we were held up at a roadblock, yadda yadda."

"We'll get arrested."

"And we take it from there. Two, we slip round the south side of the hill where there is a lot of shrubbery for cover, and try to scale the wall."

"We'll die."

"Third and last option, we drive up and use some excuse to get them to let us in."

"How good is your Spanish?"

"Good enough to pretend I am a recent immigrant to the European Union from Eastern Europe. But I am bilingual in Farsi. And we have the uniforms."

"Jesus, Gallin! It's suicide."

"OK, we'll go with your plan. Oh, wait, you haven't got one."

"OK, so you're an Iranian captain and I'm a Russian recruit. My Russian is good enough."

"Why are you wearing an Iranian uniform?"

"I've been seconded."

She grunted. "Just try not to talk. So they let us in, what then?"

I thought about it for a moment, and the seed of an idea began to dawn. "That was Manuel Torreras who received him at the airport, right?" She nodded. "That's what someone coming to negotiate a deal for an oil consortium might expect. So that's what they'd do to allay suspicion."

"OK..."

"But what they really wanted was to take him into custody because somebody, either in Russia or Iran, suspects he is heading some agency related to Central Intelligence."

"That's pretty much what we talked about last night, yes."

"So we are part of the interrogation team."

"Torreras knows you."

"But he doesn't know you, and in any case we have no reason to see Torreras. We have our brief."

"Where?" I stared at her. She shook her head. "We'll need to show them something, a document, orders..."

I pulled my last burner from my pocket and called Lovelock. After the formalities of identification I told her, "I need an electronic pass on my cell to allow me access to interrogate Nero. A Russian pass."

"To what?"

"He's been arrested. We need access to him to get him

out. Or at least to know what his plan is. I have no clue what he is playing at, Lovelock."

There was a protracted silence. After a moment her voice came to me, slightly unsteady. "I'll get the techs to fix you something. How soon do you need it?"

"As soon as possible, Lovelock. It's seven AM here. He's been locked up at Almodóvar Castle since four AM."

"I'll get back to you as soon as I can."

————

Earlier, while Nero slept and the red sun crept up on the horizon, another plane had landed in the new Republic of Andalusia. It was not a Gulfstream and it had not landed in Malaga. It was an Ilyushin Il-76, especially adapted for transporting high-ranking military brass and politicians on long-haul flights across Russia. It landed in Seville, and its single passenger was met by President Benjamin Musa's private Mercedes S class limousine.

It was a tableau that was curiously tragic: the fat plane sitting in the darkness of the empty airport, in a pool of desolate light, the single, slightly hunched figure making her unsteady way down the steps toward the two uniformed men who awaited her beside the single car. Behind them dull light glowed in only one window of the vast, glass and steel building.

The colonel who met her saluted smartly. Vitsin acknowledged the salute with a nod, and asked in English, "Where is he?"

"He is in Almodovar, Colonel. It is a fortress and there is no escape. It is an hour and a half from here."

"What does he know?"

"Nothing, Colonel Vitsin. He believes he is due to meet the president today, and negotiate with the president and Mr. Torreras. At the moment he is sleeping."

"Good. Take me there."

"The president has asked that you take breakfast with him at the palace."

Frustration bordering on rage clawed at her belly. She bit back the invective that sprang to her nicotine-stained lips and spat, "Half an hour! I have no time to waste!"

She pushed past the officers and walked with rapid, jerky steps to the car. The captain hurried to get the door, but she had climbed in already. She had learnt long ago that the trappings of power had little to do with power itself and served usually to conceal weakness. The colonel climbed in beside her and the captain climbed behind the wheel. As they pulled out of the darkened airport, Colonel Vitsin sneered privately to herself. *Who had the trappings?* she asked herself, *and who had the power?*

EIGHTEEN

Nero's eyes snapped open. He struggled to roll to the side of the bed and levered himself into a sitting position. From his luggage he recovered his toilet bag and then walked a little unsteadily to the bathroom, where he showered, lathering himself from head to foot until he looked like an abominable snowman, before rinsing himself clean and toweling himself dry. After that he took his time shaving and applying various pungent unguents to his face, body and hair, and finally he set fastidiously about dressing. The whole operation took, as he had known it would, exactly one hour.

At ten o'clock there was a tap on the door. A moment later it opened and a man in a white jacket and white gloves wheeled in a trolley bearing coffee, a basket of croissants and a number of dishes covered with silver domes. The man unloaded the dishes onto a table, bowed and was about to leave. Nero halted him.

"*Habla ingles?*"

The man nodded. "Yes, I speak English, *señor*."

"You will please inform Mr. Torreras that neither he nor I can afford to waste any more time. I require to speak to him and President Musa in the next half hour."

The man bowed and left, locking the door behind him. Shortly after that two maids came to clean his chambers, while he sat in the living room reading Walt Whitman and muttering, "Bloody lists."

And at half past ten there was another tap at the door and it opened to reveal Manuel Torreras, the Minister for Oil, and a woman in a skirt and a jacket of a color that lingered nameless between brown and green. She wore a blouse that had once been cream, thick tights and men's brown leather slip-on shoes. Nero observed her closely and noted she wore no makeup. Her hair had once been blonde, but was now turning to gray without putting up a fight. It was pulled back tight into a ponytail and secured with a simple elastic band. Her skin was pallid and unhealthy. The whites of her eyes were yellow and her lips were thin and straight. She had the face, thought Nero, of a sadist.

Manuel Torreras simpered. His head and his glasses glinted in the light from the window.

"I have brought a friend, Mr. Nero. She would very much like to speak with you."

Nero's voice snapped out like a gunshot. "I am here, Mr. Torreras, to speak with President Musa! I am not here to play games and chitchat with your friends!"

The woman spoke. "I am Colonel Alexandrina Vitsin, Mr. Nero. I have known you for many years now. And you are here to talk to me." She turned to Torreras. "Go."

He bowed. "I will leave two men outside the door."

She ignored him and he left. The colonel stepped to an armchair opposite Nero and sat. She watched him closely while she extracted a packet of cigarettes from her jacket. She picked one free with nicotine-stained fingers from which the nails had been chewed away. She did not avert her eyes even as she lit up and dragged the smoke deep into her lungs. It was like being stared down by a skeleton, Nero thought, from whom everything but the outer skin had rotted away. She spoke as she exhaled the smoke.

"I have been looking for you for a very long time, Mr. Nero."

"A fruitless quest, madam. I am nobody."

"You are a liar. Explain to me, I do not understand, why are you here?"

Nero sighed, snapped his book shut, and laid it by his side. Finally he gestured at her. "Because you have lured me here."

She gave her head a small shake. Smoke coiled up from her cigarette, making her right eye squint. "I have been hunting for you since your intervention on Elizabeth Island. But every time I have reached for you, you have slipped away. Now, you walk easily into a trap you must have seen from the beginning. Why?"

"That is a stupid question. The stakes have never been this high. If Europe is dragged into an internal war, the USA will be forced to intervene. The cost in terms of the balance of power will be devastating to the West. You know this full well. It is the very reason you have engineered this war."

Her smile was cruel, as thin as a poisonous worm. "Your Afghanistan, your Ukraine."

"No doubt that was how you thought of it. But the fact

is, madam, that however crude and obvious your plan may be, it worked, and when I saw that you were attempting to lure me here, I acceded for the purpose of negotiating. I offer myself in exchange for an end to this bid for independence."

The colonel showed her yellow teeth. "I do not believe that you are this naïve."

"There is no oil, is there?"

She barked a laugh. "Ha! That is foolish!"

"The equipment is sent from the factory in Russia. It has the false data already programmed into it. When the data seemed to show deep, low-lying reserves, you offered the machinery to extract it, and activated your sleepers to sue for independence. But there is no oil, is there?"

She was still smiling, but her eyes had become hooded. "We are not here for you to ask questions, Mr. Nero. You are here to answer my questions." She sat forward, with her elbows on her scrawny knees. It was an oddly manly gesture. "But I will answer you. Yes, Mr. Nero, there is oil. Oil is real, and Arab, Islamic socialism will spread into southern Iberia and Europe, with Russian help, seeking that oil—and will begin to infect Catalonia and France. Already there are many millions of Muslims in France." She narrowed her eyes further and her laugh came like a rank, fetid hiss through her yellow teeth. "Western democracy is infected, Mr. Nero, it is black and rotting and falling apart before your eyes, and there is nothing you can do to save it."

Nero waited until her laughter had faded. "What can I do," he asked finally, "that will persuade you to pull back from a civil war in Spain?"

"Nothing. And if you came here in that hope, I am disappointed, Mr. Nero. I thought of you as formidable man, with formidable mind. But it seems you are just fat stupid."

"I can give you everything relating to the CIA, I can give you the entire structure of the Five Eyes network, I can provide you with codes from the NSA and from British GCHQ."

"I don't believe you. We know your system in West is compartmentalized."

"But everything, *everything*, passes through me. I am at the center, and I control everything. I am the Director of Intelligence Networks, and I can tell you everything there is to know about Western Intelligence."

She crushed out the stub of her cigarette in a glass ashtray on the coffee table and fished another from her pack. She placed it between her thin lips and lit it, releasing the smoke in clouds around her face as she spoke.

"We can get that from you anyway, Mr. Nero. I don't think you have much resistance to pain."

"You would be surprised, and by the time I gave you the information it would be obsolete, and Western Intelligence would have had the biggest review in modern history. You would be back to square one."

"We see. Directorate of Intelligence Networks. You are Pentagon? NATO? You are a branch of CIA?"

"Call off the war, madam! Tell Musa to offer a truce, a negotiation! Then I will tell you everything."

All the humor drained from her face. "You know what I think, Mr. Nero? I think your ultra-secret department is you. Without you, your department is nothing. And I think when you are dead, or broken, and Western economy has collapsed because of war in Spain and infestation of Islam, I think it will not matter if you give me information or not. Because then Russia will dominate world economy again, with army that can crush Ukraine, Poland, Czech Republic, Slovakia and all the way to Germany. I want your information, Mr. Nero, but I don't need it. All I need is to break you." She sneered, "Maybe all I need is to make you hungry, uh, Mr. Fat?"

She shrieked, dilating her nostrils and opening her mouth wider than seemed possible. It was a horrible sound, like a manic parrot, or a skinny dinosaur.

"They have here, in this castle, Mr. Nero, a museum. It is in the dungeon. It has all instruments for torture from history. I think maybe we take you down to dungeon, and we see how good mediaeval people was in making interrogation."

"Information gathered under torture, madam, is notoriously unreliable."

She smiled. "I don't care, Mr. Nero. I just want to see big, fat, stupid man crying like little child."

Nero did not answer. After a moment she sucked on her cigarette and asked him, "You have something interesting to tell me, Mr. Nero? Shall we talk longer, or shall we go down, and see the museum?"

He licked his lips and drew breath, but before he could speak there was a tap at the door. The colonel's face contracted with anger and she snapped, "*What?*"

The door opened and Captain Garcia stepped in.

"Colonel, there is a Captain Hakimi downstairs, accompanied by an SVR officer, Colonel Ustinov. They are waiting downstairs. The SVR officer has orders from Moscow to interrogate the prisoner, Mr. Nero."

Colonel Vitsin's face turned the color of old parchment. "How?" she said, staring at Garcia. Her lips, stretched tight in a grimace, nevertheless trembled. Her cigarette traveled toward her face but gave up halfway. "Moscow? Ustinov? I don't know *Ustinov!*"

"They insist on coming up, ma'am."

"Send them up!"

Captain Garcia left and Vitsin sat in silence, staring at Nero. She smoked compulsively and her hand shook. After five minutes she narrowed her eyes and hissed, "Is this you?"

Nero arched an eyebrow. "I have no idea what you are saying, madam, or how I can possibly answer your question. This is me, indeed! But your question is meaningless."

She seemed not to hear him but narrowed her eyes further. "But *how?*" It was almost a whisper.

Nero sighed heavily. "Madam, if you seek a meaningful dialogue, I suggest you make statements, or ask questions which are meaningful. I cannot participate in this hissing and yammering of yours. Talk sense!"

Two pink spots appeared on her cheeks. They surprised Nero. She stood on skeletal, unsteady legs. "Tell me!" she rasped. "You were responsible for Victoria Island." His nod was almost imperceptible. "And the nuclear device that was placed in New York..."

"What good does this do you, Colonel?"

"It was you, always you, in the shadows."

"Like yourself."

"No," she shook her head, "not like me. Look at you, fat, lazy, decadent. I have you in my power. I will extract every fact, every word from you, while your Western empire crumbles around your ears."

Nero smiled. "The way the Soviet Union collapsed around yours, Colonel Vitsin? I don't think so. This war you are trying to engineer is built on lies. It is a fire made of paper. It will burn itself out and become nothing but insubstantial ashes."

She curled her lip. "What is your department? How do you operate? Who are you attached to? Talk to me or I will..."

There was a rap on the door. Her face twisted with poisonous rage and she turned and screamed, "*What? Come!*"

Captain Garcia stepped through the door. "Captain Hakimi and Colonel Ustinov of the SVR, Colonel."

NINETEEN

I AM NOT SURE WHAT I HAD EXPECTED TO FIND when the door opened, but whatever it was, it was not that woman. She stood, trembling slightly on scrawny legs, with small, ugly eyes dissecting me from a cadaverous skull.

"You are not Russian," she said.

I smiled with the kind of contempt you'd expect from an officer of the SVR. Captain Garcia had told me that Mr. Nero was with Colonel Alexandrina Vitsin, so I gave her the once-over and resisted the temptation to adopt a Hollywood Russian accent. I said, "Colonel Alexandrina Vitsin. Moscow has the greatest confidence in you..." I let the words linger just long enough as I arched an eyebrow. "But they sent me along to oversee your operation. Just in case."

Then I turned to Nero, who was watching me like he wanted to slap me, with a baseball bat.

"Mr. Nero, at last. You are a hard man to get a hold of."

He turned to Vitsin. "Two things have become abundantly clear, madam. This absurd bid for independence by

Andalusia is, as I suspected from the start, entirely a Russian fabrication stage-managed from Moscow, and Russia continues to be as bumbling, foolish and incompetent as the Soviet Union was in its day. My dear lady, you could not, as the English say, organize a piss up in a brewery!"

She turned on him with real fury. Two red dots burned on her cheeks. I cut her short before she could speak.

"I see your reputation does you justice, Mr. Nero. You are as arrogant and insolent as I expected."

Vitsin turned on me like a viper. "Reputation? *Reputation?*" She pointed a trembling hand at Nero. "When have you heard of this man? *What information have you about this man?*"

Nero's arched eyebrow told me I had screwed up, but I wasn't about to let on. I barked a contemptuous laugh. "My dear Vitsin! After your catalogue of failures and your history of incompetence, did you really believe the Kremlin was going to sit by and allow you to continue wasting resources while achieving nothing? Oh no, we have had Mr. Nero in our sights for a while now." I turned to Nero. "And now, Mr. Nero, it is time for you to answer some questions. There are some people in Moscow who are very keen to meet you."

Vitsin whirled on me and screamed, "*What?*"

"The prisoner comes with me to Moscow, Colonel."

She stepped up to me. The smell of stale tobacco was strong on her breath. "Show me your orders!"

"On what authority do you demand to see my orders?"

"This is *my* operation! I conceived it! I discussed it with the president himself!"

"And *he* called me and instructed me to keep an eye on you so you would not screw up *again!*"

She became hysterical, pointing at me furiously and giving little jumps as she screamed, "*You see? You see? You are fake! You are impostor! I never spoke to Putin! I never discussed this operation with him! You lie! You are a liar and an impostor!*"

I opened my mouth to laugh at her and refute her claim, but Gallin stepped forward and delivered that devastating right hook of hers again. Colonel Vitsin sprawled on the floor with her twiggy legs at odd angles. Then she turned calmly to Captain Garcia and said, "*Arreste a esta mujer. Es impostora. Hay que comprobar sus papeles.*"

Garcia stood with a slack jaw, frowning at her. She had told him to arrest Vitsin whole we checked her papers, because she was an impostor. He was so far out of his depth he wasn't even treading water anymore, and when soldiers feel that way their instinct drives them to consult a superior officer. I didn't think we needed that. So I stepped toward him, making like I was pulling papers from my inside pocket, and jabbed him hard on the tip of his chin.

I caught him before he hit the floor and laid him out gently on the floor, so as not to alert the guards outside.

Nero watched us drag them into the bedroom, tie them up and gag them. When we were done and returned to the living room, he said, "What, in the name of all that is unholy, are you doing?"

I felt a small stab of irritation and said, "Rescuing you, sir."

"And what, Alex, makes you think I need rescuing? Your instructions were perfectly clear. I do not recall at any time telling you that I needed rescuing."

Gallin cut in. "With all due respect, sir. You look to me like you need rescuing."

He didn't answer her. He returned his gaze to me. "Have you any idea how long I have been after that woman?"

I nodded. "Yeah, since we met on Victoria Island. So now you have her."

"And how exactly, Alex, do you propose we get her back to Arlington?"

I shrugged. I was beginning to feel sheepish about our short-term planning in the last few hours. "Well, how were *you* planning to get her back?"

"Because I, Alex, had planned ahead. I have contacts in Moscow who were due to broadcast Russia's lies to Spain about the oil reserves, and her unholy alliance with Iran. Your job was to provide evidence of those two facts. While I was extracted from Moscow, with Vitsin as my prisoner."

"You didn't exactly make that clear, sir."

"Are you telling me this fracas is my fault, Alex?"

"No."

"I seem to remember making it clear that York had compromised communications."

"Yes."

"I do not recall at any time telling you to rescue me."

"No."

Gallin was getting antsy. "The reality show is fun and all, but we need to be getting the hell out of here."

Nero turned to her. "That does not solve our problem, Captain Gallin. Yours and Mr. Mason's very clear instructions were to gather evidence of the Russian and Iranian involvement in this conflict, including the reliability of the reports on the oil reserves, so that we could defuse this civil war before it erupts. Escaping from this calamitous situation will not—"

"Sir," I interrupted. "Sitting here making unnecessarily long sentences will not help either. We take her and we go. If she was involved in engineering this war, and she knew about your existence, then she will probably know if the reports are fake."

"If, if and probably. That is not satisfactory."

"Sir, we have to go because if we don't we will probably be killed very shortly."

Gallin added, "There is a good chance they are checking with Moscow right now to verify the electronic documents Lovelock sent us."

He grunted, sighed heavily and levered himself to his feet. "We take Colonel Vitsin. We go to Gibraltar."

I went to the door and wrenched it open. The two guards snapped to attention. I addressed the one who looked oldest. "Manuel Torreras, the Minister for Oil, tell him we need him now!"

"He is no here, señor. He go back to Malaga."

I thought about it a moment and went back inside.

"Sir, you and Gallin take Vitsin to Gibraltar."

"What do you intend to do?"

"If anyone can prove the oil reports are fake, it's Dr Montilla. I have to go get him and his data."

He nodded. "Very well, let's see if we can get out of this damned castle alive."

While Gallin dumped Captain Garcia in the bed, wrapped him in three sheets, tied him with his bootlaces and his belt, I poked my head out of the door and snapped, "Get two Land Rovers ready. We are taking the prisoner to

Malaga."

The one I had spoken to earlier saluted and went off at the hurry up to arrange the trucks. I turned to the other one. "You, Captain Garcia is in conversation with Moscow. Go, do not disturb him."

He saluted too and went after his pal. I gave Gallin the nod and she came out with Nero, with his hands behind his back. I went in and grabbed Colonel Vitsin. She was pretty groggy from the right hook Gallin had given her, but when I showed her the Glock 17 I'd taken from Captain Garcia her eyes focused.

"The minister has returned to Malaga. Garcia is trussed up in bed with a gag the size of Ukraine in his mouth. That leaves a handful of men downstairs who believe I am an envoy from Moscow. Now, you will understand that my position right now is desperate, and desperate men do desperate things. Your best bet for surviving the next three hours is to shut up and do as you're told. Because if you give me one problem, just one small problem, I will blow your nasty little brain right out of your nasty little skull. Do we understand each other, Colonel?" She nodded. I said, "Stand up and walk."

I folded my jacket over my arm so it covered the Glock, made her slip her hand through my elbow and shoved the semi-automatic in her side. Then we followed Nero and Gallin down the sandstone stairs to the entrance hall. We were headed for the door, which stood open onto the large, cobbled yard where the Land Rovers stood in the midmorning sunshine, when I heard a voice behind me.

"Colonel Ustinov." I turned. It was a man in his mid

thirties dressed in the uniform of a lieutenant in the Guardia Civil. "Where are you taking the prisoner?"

"I am taking him to Malaga and then to Moscow. How is that any of your business?"

"I was instructed by Seville to secure this facility and to receive a prisoner. I was instructed that Colonel Vitsin would conduct the interrogation here. Nobody has informed me about you, Colonel Ustinov, or that the prisoner was to be transported."

I shook my head. "I cannot be responsible for incompetence in your channels of communication, Lieutenant. As you can see, Colonel Vitsin is accompanying me and the prisoner. Do you plan to arrest us because you have not received instructions from your superiors?"

He blinked a couple of times at me, then shifted his gaze to Vitsin. I pressed the muzzle of the pistol hard into her side. She said, "I will ensure you receive the proper authorization, Lieutenant."

We stepped out into the sunshine, where we shoved Nero in the back of the lead Land Rover and Vitsin in the front passenger seat next to Gallin, who was at the wheel. I climbed in the rear Land Rover and we fired up the engines. The huge castle doors began to swing open and in my wing mirror I saw the lieutenant step out of the building. He weas watching us like a hawk and I could tell by his eyes and by the set of his mouth, that he was searching for a reason to give the order to close the doors and have us shot.

The gap was wide enough and Gallin put her truck in gear. Next thing she was roaring out leaving a cloud of dust behind her. I went after her and all the way down the hill. I had my eyes on the mirror, waiting for the pursuit. It didn't come.

Not then.

We drove fast, heading first west, toward Seville, but after just twenty miles we turned south, cutting through dry fields and olive groves on remote, country roads, climbing, after Ecija, into high sierras with dense pinewoods among parched fields of olive groves. The roads were empty, as were the fields. Even in that desolation the imminent presence of violence was palpable. It seemed to lurk, invisible in the vast blue sky, or in the dark shadows among the pine trees and the olive groves.

We eventually pulled into a patch of scrubland beside the railway station outside the village of Bobadilla. There we bound and gagged Vitsin and laid her on the floor in the back of the truck. Meanwhile Nero called the Governor of Gibraltar to arrange for a diplomatic reception at La Linea, to receive them and escort them in to Gibraltar. The governor must have asked him what a diplomatic reception was, because I heard Nero sigh and speak very deliberately.

"David, I am extremely tired and in something of a pickle. Please don't tax me with niceties. Make whatever arrangements you need to make, but when we arrive at La Linea, please enfold us in your diplomatic cloak, and escort us in to Gibraltar. We are about eighty miles away." He paused a moment, listening, then said, "Kindly do a little more than see what you can manage. Get me through and we may just manage to avert a European war."

While he was talking I stepped aside with Gallin. She punched me gently on the chest. "My orders were to stay with you."

"Nero can do a lot of things, but he can't do this without your help. If they stop him at a roadblock, he'll get snooty, correct their grammar and lecture them on Spanish history."

"What about you? You going to be OK? I feel..." She faltered and shrugged. "I'm supposed to be doing this with you."

I smiled. "We will always have Malaga. We didn't have. We'd lost it, but we got it back last night."

She gave a little laugh. "Jerk. What are you going to do?"

"I'm going to look for Torreras, or better still Montilla. If Nero is right about those wells, I need to get the evidence to prove it. If we can show the Russians have lied to the Andalusian people, the whole independence movement will fall apart, and the Russian-Iranian-Andalusian alliance with it."

"I'll leave Nero and Vitsin at the border and come and find you."

"Where I'm going you can't go. What I have to do you can't be any part of."

"Cut it out. I'll call you in a couple of hours." I nodded. She punched me softly on the chest again. "Stay safe, buddy."

I watched them drive away, to the south and the west, and when they had disappeared from view I climbed into my truck and headed east, toward Malaga. I knew any attempt to contact Manuel Torreras would be fatal. But I might just pull off a meeting with Dr. Montilla. His cell number would be easy to find on the University of Malaga website. All I needed was a credible identity and a credible excuse for a meeting.

I drove slowly, scrolling through my last burner looking for the Malaga University website. I found it and after a couple of minutes I found Montilla, his e-mail, his landline and his cell.

I called. *"Si, dígame?"*

"Dr Montilla? This is Dr. Abramovitch, of the University of Moscow."

"Oh, Doctor, how do you do? How can I help you?"

"It is rather a delicate matter, Dr. Montilla, and a little urgent. We are conducting research, it is somewhat complicated, concerning fossil remains and the period of the Younger Dryas. You have heard of it?"

Naturally."

"It is a matter of some complexity and I know there are people in Moscow who would like us, you and I, to cooperate as a means of giving legitimacy to the drilling for oil at such a sensitive time for our climate, you understand."

There was a pause. This was unexpected. He hesitated a moment, then: "Yes, I see, well, how can I help you, Dr. Abramovich? What kind of cooperation? I am a very busy man."

I gave a small laugh. "Of course. I do understand and I will take as little of your time as I am able. I wonder if we could meet briefly this evening." I gave a small laugh. "Time is of course of the essence at the moment."

"Yes, well, where are you? I am in Malaga at the moment."

"Perfect, I am in Malaga too. Allow me to take you to lunch. Where shall we meet?" Before he could answer, I drove on. "I'll tell you what! Let's meet at the lighthouse. I can park up there and we'll have lunch at the port. There are one or two places that are still open there, I think."

The parking lot at the lighthouse suited me because it gave me plenty of cover from which I could watch him arrive, and approach him unseen. But he didn't like it.

"No, I have a better idea, Dr. Abramovich. I am almost finished in town, and, as you will appreciate, I am keen to get out of the city. Come to my house in the *Montes de Málaga*. We'll relax over a late lunch, and if those bastards in Spain start bombing us, we can have dinner too and you can stay in one of the guest rooms. We will not be a prime target. Are you staying at the Hyatt? I think it's the only hotel that is still open. I will send my driver for you."

I thanked him and hung up, and smiled to myself. My only remaining problem was that he'd met me and he knew me, and that was not going to be easy to get around.

TWENTY

I FIGURED THE ONE PLACE THE COPS WOULD NOT BE looking for me—if they were looking for me at all—would be at my hotel. So I dumped the Land Rover in a back street and covered the last couple of miles to the port on foot. I didn't go into the hotel when I got there. I waited outside on the steps.

At three thirty my cell rang. It had to be either Nero, Gallin or Montilla. Nobody else had that number. It turned out to be neither. It was a voice like a snake's if a snake could talk.

"Mr. Abramovich?"

"Speaking."

"I am Rinpoche, Dr. Montilla's personal servant. I am arriving at the hotel in two minutes. I wait downstairs in a dark Mercedes."

I smiled. It's either an Audi or a Mercedes. Something to do with the criminal mind. "I'm waiting on the steps," I told him.

He was tall, skinny and lanky, and had the very short hair and indefinable air that a lot of Buddhists have. He parked at the bottom of the steps and held the door of the car open for me.

As we pulled out onto the avenue and turned east, I asked him, "Rinpoche, isn't that a Tibetan monk?"

He hunched his shoulders and grinned with broken teeth at the mirror.

"Is a nickname. What to do?"

We travelled along the coast for twenty minutes, then came off the highway and turned inland. We came to a road-block fortified with sandbags and a heavy machine gun, but they waved us through and I noticed he had a sticker on the windshield. I pointed to it.

"Is that a pass?"

"Dr. Montilla must travel all over Andalusia. He must have a priority pass."

The road snaked, climbing high into the hills. The sun began to slip behind the arid hills of red earth, olives and avocado plantations. Soon, even those fell away and we were high in the *Sierra de Tejeda*, where pines and gnarled cypress bushes fought for survival against the dust and the crippling heat of the sun.

And suddenly I was aware of the remoteness of where I was going, and with that awareness came an awareness that death was riding with me in that car. I looked at Rinpoche and saw he was studying me in the mirror. His face, lit by the copper light of the declining sun, wasn't even expressionless.

"Are you a Buddhist, Rinpoche?"

He laughed. "Why do you ask me this?"

I shrugged. "Why else would you have that nickname? Also, you look like a Buddhist."

"Do you work for Dr. Montilla? Or are you seconded to him from Russia?"

He kept smiling his impassive smile at the road. I wondered if he was a Slav, or a Cossack. He said nothing and after a bit I said, "You're not going to answer me?"

He showed his broken teeth to the windshield. "What to tell? What to do?"

I sighed and turned to look at the wild hills outside. We passed small villages with names that did not sound Spanish: Sayalonga, Archez, Daimalo. The sense of remoteness grew and after an hour we came to a valley at the foot of a huge hulk of a mountain. Rinpoche laughed for no apparent reason and pointed.

"La Maroma," he said. "Ghosts, spirits and even some gods living in there. Biggest mountain in the Sierra of Tejeda. Big, fat mountain."

We passed the tiny village of Salares and turned right onto a broad dirt track. We bumped and lurched over the rough, uneven surface, twisting and climbing for another twenty minutes into deep pine forest. Finally, we came off the broad track and onto a narrower path through the trees and crested the hill. Now the track cut straight through a rough landscape of gnarled bushes, dry weeds and rocks to a dry stone wall with an iron gate. Beside the gate was a large blue and white tile with an image of the Buddha sitting on a lotus flower. It had an inscription that read, *Nirvana*.

I looked at Rinpoche's reflection as the gate swung slowly open. I had a strange feeling that I had strayed out of my depth.

"Are you going to kill me?"

He turned his reptilian smile on me, full of detached amusement.

"Today, I am not killing anybody."

We held each other's gazes for a few moments. I knew he was calibrating me, visualizing the best way to kill me when the time came. How had Montilla known? Then it dawned on me. Montilla had been a party to the deception. He knew there was no oil. So equally he would have known that Moscow was not going to send a Dr. Abramovich to legitimize the extraction. That's why he'd sent this freak show to collect me, and that was why he had brought me to this remote location. I smiled.

"That's very comforting." Silently I told him I could make the same promise. His eyes creased and he laughed, like he'd read my thoughts. He put the car in gear and we rolled through the gates.

The house was large and set among exotic gardens of succulents, palms and cacti that would not have looked out of place in Arizona. The sun had dipped behind La Maroma and the pine trees, sixty or seventy yards to the west of the house, were casting long shadows across the arid land and the paved, balustraded terrace where a turquoise pool lapped and sploshed, like there was no civil war about to erupt.

Rinpoche pulled up where three broad steps led up to the pool. I climbed out of the car and stood looking. It was very still in the heat. The only sound, aside from the lap of the pool, was the sawing of the cicadas.

The house was built to look like a castle, with towers at the corners and a massive rotunda at the center, bulging against the blue-white sky. Rinpoche sat on the hood of the car and crossed his arms.

"He is inside."

I crossed the paved terrace to the entrance. It was a stone arch with heavy wooden doors. I hammered on it and heard footsteps approaching from inside and the door swung open. I don't know if they have Bigfoot in Russia, but if they have, I'm pretty sure Putin sent Dr. Montilla one as a gift. He was wearing a white jacket that looked like it might explode at any moment. He grunted softly and turned away. I followed him across a large room with heavy wooden furniture and an open fireplace, down a passage tiled in terracotta, around a dogleg and finally came to another castle door with iron studs in it. Bigfoot knocked with a fist the size of five small, hairy people and stepped inside.

His voice was like the grinding of tectonic plates: "Dr. Abramovich."

I stepped inside, with a fixed smile on my face, and the primal humanoid closed the door.

Dr. Montilla was sitting at a small, collapsible table in the middle of the room. The room looked like a library, with books on every wall from floor to ceiling. There was a desk and an open fireplace that gave the air a hint of soot. Montilla's table was covered in a white, linen tablecloth. There was a bottle of what looked like champagne beside the table in a silver ice bucket, and on the table there were two plates, two crystal champagne glasses and two white, linen napkins. His napkin was stuffed in his shirt, and his glass was more than half full. His small, round glasses glinted in the dying light from the window as he scooped caviar from a silver dish and spread it on a cracker which he had taken from a wicker basket. He spoke without looking at me.

"Which was the lie, Abramovich or Mason?" Before I could answer he went on. "Which was the trap, a test of loyalty or attempted espionage? Please sit."

I sat and pulled the bottle from the ice bucket. "Krug Clos d'Ambonnay, '98, and real Russian caviar. With that kind of rewards, I figure Moscow already gave you the answer to your questions."

He still wasn't looking at me. His small, glinting lenses were focused on his next cracker, which he was smearing with slimy black eggs.

"You were not to know, Mr. Mason, but not only have I an exceptional memory for voices, but your reason for wanting to see me was as ridiculous as it was inventive."

I pored myself some champagne and sipped it. It was exceptional. I said, "There is no oil, is there?"

That surprised him and he finally looked at me. I still couldn't see his eyes, hidden behind the reflection of the window behind me. I went on, "If there was no oil, Moscow would not be concerned about legitimizing the drilling. The oil was only ever a hook to encourage the Andalusian people to vote for independence. Are you Spanish, Dr. Montilla?"

He snorted, then sipped. "Spanish? What is Spanish, Mr. Mason? Iberian? Roman? Moroccan? Berber? Arab? Or perhaps Celtic, Germanic or Basque. Or Jewish! The bulk of the Andalusian population, five or six hundred years ago, was Jewish. My name, Montilla, suggests I am descended from Jews. What does it mean, to be Jewish, to be Spanish, to be Russian? You ask me this question, am I Spanish? But what does it mean?"

"For some people it is a focus for loyalty and patriotism, it symbolizes a standard to which they hold themselves."

He threw back his head and shrieked with laughter. "Loyalty. Loyalty must be a two-way street, Mr. Mason, otherwise it is mere obedience. And patriotism is a mere fantasy devised by people like me to make people feel good about their obedience. Do you know what the word 'Islam' means in Arabic, Mr. Mason?"

"Subjugation."

"Good." He nodded approval. "Very good. Islam is extraordinarily clever at making people feel good about being obedient. If I may paraphrase John, greater obedience hath no man than this, that he will lay down his life for his master."

"What about you? You lay down the lives of innocent men, women and children—"

"Innocent? Innocent of what, precisely?"

"Fine, men, women and innocent children, for what? For a political ideology? So that Russia and China can become the dominant powers on the Earth?"

He gestured with both hands at the caviar. "Please, please, eat, drink. I am eating it all myself!" I sipped and he shook his head. "I have no political ideology, Mr. Mason. Frankly, I don't give a damn about anything except my own, greedy pleasures. Benjamin Musa, Alvaro Romero, they hunger for power and dance to Moscow's tune. For me it is merely a matter of money. I want money, lots and lots of money."

"It doesn't trouble you that, if this war erupts, people will die, children will lose their parents and be killed?"

He watched me through his glinting lenses and the corners of his mouth twitched.

"Oh, stop, you will break my heart!" And he threw back his head and screamed with laughter again.

His laughter subsided and he scooped some more slimy, black eggs onto a cracker.

"There is nothing either good or bad, but thinking makes it so. Hamlet, act two, scene two." He stuffed the cracker in his mouth and spoke with his mouth full. "True freedom is freedom from the illusion of morality, from the belief that there is good and evil. There is only power, Mr. Mason."

"Even if you are right, Dr. Montilla, you and your philosophy disgust me. And I think a mind like yours, obsessed with its own power and satisfaction, to the exclusion of all other people, is a sick, impoverished mind."

A flicker of anger contracted his face.

"Do you know, Mr. Mason, what Yahweh means?"

"I'm pretty sure you're about to tell me."

His face turned suddenly vicious and strings of spittle sprayed from his pink lips. "Forgive me if I bore you! But I shall tell you anyway, for your edification! When God, known until then only as Elohim, appeared to Moses as the burning bush and told him to lead the Jews to the promised land, Moses asked him, 'What shall I tell them is your name?' And Elohim said, 'Tell them my name is, Ehyeh.' In Hebrew this means, 'I am.' But Moses said to God, 'They will not understand this,' so God said, 'Very well, then tell them my name is Yahweh.' Which means, 'He is.' And so, the god Yahweh was born."

"What's your point?"

"Humanity was offered the truth that each one of us is God. God is 'I Am.' But in their craven cowardice and stupidity they chose to project God onto a leader, a prophet, a guide—anyone but themselves. In this simple act they abdicated their power and they opened the doors to the despots and the tyrants. The sheep are happy to be slaughtered, if the Lord ordains it."

"Did you bring me here to quote Shakespeare and the Bible at me, or are your storm troopers about to burst in and shoot me?"

"No storm troopers, Mr. Mason. I was curious to discover if it was indeed you. I was also curious to discover what you wanted. This war will be protracted. Moscow wants to punch a hole in the Western economy, as you have deduced, and the best way to do that is to embroil Europe and America in a never-ending war. As the CIA did with the Soviet Union in Afghanistan, and later with Russia in Ukraine."

"Yeah, I had got that far."

He stuffed the last of his caviar in his mouth, swallowed it with a smug little smile, and sipped his champagne.

"So, the question becomes, how much will the USA pay me to blow the whistle and prove there is no oil in Spain?"

That took me by surprise. I arched an eyebrow and sipped more champagne. As I set down the glass I told him, "Nothing."

He became serious. "You are joking. This information is worth billions."

I shook my head. "Only if you have proof. And there is no way you can prove that."

He leaned back in his chair, studying my face. He held

his glass in his right hand and cupped his right elbow in his left hand. It was a curiously feminine gesture.

"What could be better proof than the testimony of the geologist placed in charge of finding the oil?"

"Plenty. Musa would say you were lying and the Russians would back him up. And that could hold at least long enough for the war to cause serious damage to the Western economy. If you are going to be of any value, it has to be with concrete, irrefutable proof."

He arched an eyebrow and looked amused. "And what sort of proof would that be? No doubt when you called me you had some kind of proof in mind which you intended to steal from me."

I nodded and took another pull on my champagne before refilling my glass. "Yeah, data, a hard drive, software, something forensic that could not be falsified."

"And did you think we would strike some kind of deal, or did you plan to steal it?"

"The plan was flexible and open to improvisation. I could not identify the forensic evidence on my own, but I didn't think you'd be to hard to convince. Losing a kneecap without anesthetic can make people pretty helpful. It's like what you were saying about Islam."

His eyes creased and his cheeks seemed to swell. His body wobbled with silent laughter.

"I am sure we can reach an understanding, Mr. Mason, without the need for surgery."

"Good, what can you offer me?"

"Aside from the last of the champagne?" He reached over and shared the last of the Krug between us. Then he sat back in his chair again. "I can offer you an example of the data-feed boxes which altered the data being received into the main computer from the sonar. I can offer you a hard drive I installed which received the data bypassing the data-feed, I can offer you printouts before and after being processed by the Russian computers, which show that there is absolutely *nothing* under Granada and Almeria, or the Coto Doñana, but rock and earth."

I frowned. "Why did you bypass the data-feed? Why the dual printouts?"

"Because I foresaw just how valuable that information would be. How much do you think the American government will be willing to pay me for *proof* that there is no oil? One tenth of what they were going to spend on a European war would make me the richest man on the planet."

I sipped my drink and studied his face. "Where is it?"

"It here. It's in my office, and some of the larger parts are downstairs, in my basement."

A wave of weariness washed over me. For a moment my thoughts were distracted and I struggled to focus.

"So how did you plan to get these items—the data-feed boxes, the hard drive you installed which bypassed the data-feed, the printouts—how did you plan to get them to the US authorities?"

He watched me a little too long before answering. "I confess, Mr. Mason, that was a challenge, my options were to find a way into Gibraltar, or to drive across the border into Spain, which was a high-risk proposition." He trailed off, still watching me closely.

"You can't..." I paused, searching for words, wondering why I couldn't find them. I shook my head. How many hours had it been since I'd slept? It wasn't that many. But my eyes were heavy and I could see my thoughts, like rows of dominos flipping and trailing into each other in odd, irrational sequences. I would have to talk to Montilla about making his thought processes more coherent—

I snapped out of it, blinked hard and tried to focus on Montilla. He was smiling.

"You can't," I said again. "You can't go across into Spain. You'll die. They'll shoot you on sight. I can take you. Your Merc has the pass, on the windshield. We can drive. It's only a few hours to Gibraltar…"

"You look tired, Mr. Mason. You sound tired. Your eyes look heavy. You can barely keep them from closing. They look so heavy you must close them. We will drive, Mr. Mason. We will drive all the way, through the dark all-enveloping night, all the way, but first you must rest, Mr. Mason. First you must close your eyes and sleep deeply, very deeply, all the way down in the deepest part of your mind, sleep."

I had the uncomfortable feeling that somebody had spread butter on my eyeballs. I squeezed them a couple of times but it didn't help. The sleepiness was overwhelming and I could feel my will slipping away. I I knew the bastard had drugged me and I wanted to tell him he was a son of a bitch, but my tongue was too thick and wouldn't get out of the way for the words. I leaned on the table and tried to stand, but my legs folded and I crashed onto the table. It collapsed under my weight and I landed in a heap on the floor, too weak to get up. The last thing I remember seeing was Rinpoche's face grinning at me, and behind him, Montilla, smiling.

TWENTY-ONE

When I woke up, my mouth tasted like a dead rat's ass. The other half of the rat was in my belly, eating away at my stomach lining. It was awful dark and I hurt everywhere. I hurt in places I didn't even know I had. There was the musty smell of damp and slow, rotting decay. For a moment I wondered if I was dead and I had woken up in my coffin, but by degrees I became aware that my feet and my ass were on a hard, cold floor, something hard was pressing into my back and my hands were tied behind my back. And when I tried to lever myself into a standing position, I realized that whatever it was that was pressing into my back, was between me and my hands.

Slowly it dawned on me: the dark, the smell, the object pressing into my back—I was in a cellar, tied to some kind of metal pipe. And that would account also for the small rustling sounds I kept hearing. That would be the rats.

Briefly I thought about the fact that some people are crazy enough to lock you in a cellar with a bunch of rats and leave you to die slowly of hunger while the rats avoid that very fate by eating you. Montilla definitely seemed crazy enough to fit the bill, but I dismissed the thought. Not because it was unlikely, but because it was all too likely.

I struggled to my feet and tried to get a feel for the bonds on my wrists. It seemed to be fine, nylon rope of the sort you'd use for mountaineering. The sort that was designed to resist friction with sharp rocks and support hundreds of pounds of weight without breaking.

My ankles, at least, were not bound. But how I was going to free my hands in the pitch black was looking like an insurmountable problem, unless I could persuade a rat to eat through the nylon rope. But something told me my wrists would probably be a more appetizing proposition. Not to put too fine a point on it, right then, I was looking about as screwed as a two-dollar whore during shore leave.

There was a creak in the darkness, and over to my right a slash of light appeared and swelled. Within it there was a long, scrawny silhouette. I recognized it as Rinpoche. His voice traveled across the blackness. "Are we awake?"

"How long have I been unconscious?"

He giggled. It was a stupid sound and made me unreasonably mad. He said, "Oh, maybe all your life."

"Cut the guru shit, will you? How long have I been out?"

He made a small movement and a sickly yellow light snapped on overhead. It was a bare bulb under a blue plastic shade. I could see now that Rinpoche was standing at the top of a short flight of concrete steps. There were a couple of racks of wine against the bare brick walls, some wooden packing cases, an old, leather sofa with the stuffing coming out, a wooden table and four bentwood chairs.

"Maybe an hour." His voice traveled to me across the desolate space. "Your life falling apart. You feel like you are losing control. Panic is coming from feeling of losing control. Peace is coming from realizing you never had control, right?"

He giggled again and trotted down the stairs. As he approached I asked him, "Have you been instructed to torture me?"

He stood in front of me with his head on one side, grinning, showing his blackened, crooked teeth. "Torture?" he said.

"Do you think you can answer the question without coming out with some cheap, Facebook wisdom-bite?"

He seemed not to hear me. "You makin' the pain in your own brain. So you torturing yourself."

"That would be a no, then."

He pulled a large hunting knife from his belt and showed me the blade. "We are a hundred miles from Malaga. Even if you manage to escape you gonna die trying to get to town. And there are there are six guys here in the house with guns who are gonna have fun hunting you and killing you. And the closer you get to town, the more people you gonna have hunting you. So be smart. Don't try. Okay? Watcha gonna do? Right? Everything out of control. Go with the flow."

"You done with the cheap philosophy? You want to tell me what the hell is going on? One minute I'm making a deal with Montilla, the next you have me tied up in a damned dungeon."

"Always the questions. Always the questions. But never an answer. Everything always changing in the wheel of Samsara, right? So never there can be an answer. Today is right, tomorrow is wrong."

"Untie my hands. I'll show you an answer."

He giggled, creasing his eyes so they looked like they were closed. "Bound man making threats of violence."

He was fast and strong, like a whip. He started with a back-hander that almost tore my head off. Before I could respond he drove his right fist into my ribs so my lungs went into spasm and followed up with a left hook to my liver. He stood back, laughing, while I retched onto the floor. The room was spinning and my legs were trembling. Another back-hander and I was struggling to remain conscious. He could see that and started giggling again.

"Stay with me, Mason. We gotta do this journey together. Stay with me."

Somewhere in my reeling consciousness I heard the hiss of a tap. Then the icy slap of cold water brought me round.

I spluttered and blinked away the water, trying to focus on him. "What the hell do you want?"

A figure moved in the doorway at the top of the stairs. With a sick, sinking feeling I watched the simian who had opened the door to me descend the steps, removing his white jacket. Rinpoche stepped forward and grabbed my face in his right hand.

"Good," he said, "'What do you want?' is right question. That is the good news. Bad news is, answer is not coming yet. My friend Boris gonna talk to you first. He gonna talk to you in body language."

He thought that was real funny and laughed a lot. He

was still laughing when Boris started slapping my face. It was like being slapped by a blue whale. The pain was hard to believe, and as my legs sagged under me, I knew if he continued I was not going to have enough strength to escape, even if I got the chance.

I don't know if I was lucky, or if they wanted to string it out as long as possible, but he had only hit me half a dozen times, when I heard Montilla trotting down the concrete stairs. I figured it was Montilla, but I had barely the will or the strength to raise my head and look. And my face was so swollen I'm not sure I'd have been able to see him anyway.

Another bucket of cold water made me gasp and look up. Montilla was smiling, watching me.

"It gives me huge pleasure to see you like this. You are so self-assured, so arrogant, handsome, erect, with powerful shoulders. I imagine women fall at your feet continually. It is a joy—" He turned to Rinpoche and they both giggled, reaching for each other. "Such a pleasure! To see you broken like this!"

They laughed out loud and gave each other a high five.

My voice came as a feeble croak. I said, "Why? You said..." I trailed off, too exhausted to finish the question.

"Why? Because I actually *believe* in what I am doing, Mr. Mason." He laughed again, a high-pitched giggle similar to Rinpoche's. "You think I am one of these little Spanish shits? No!" He shook his head, a big grin across his shiny face. "Noi, no, no, I am Russian, Mr. Mason. And I have been many years in preparation for this mission. You think I would so easily sell out? You think I would so easily hand over all these years of my life and work, for some filthy American dollars? No, no, that is the American way. We Russians, we have soul. We are strong in our spirit. You will learn that today."

I nodded and sighed. "I am learning that, and I can see it's true. But tell me, please, what do you want? What do you want from me?"

He came up close and stared into my face, his nose barely an inch from mine. "I want two things from you, Mason; just two. I want in-for-mation, and I want you to suffer! So the longer you take to give me the information, the better for me."

Behind him Rinpoche started giggling again, and Montilla turned and grinned at him.

I said, "OK, you want to make me suffer. But I figure I have had about as much as I can take. I am not a special ops operative, Montilla. I'm an intelligence officer. They don't train us to deal with torture. Whatever it is you want to know, I am ready to talk."

"So soon? I am so disappointed. What about my fun?"

"Get it with somebody else. I am done. What do you want to know, for crying out loud?"

"It is very simple, Mason, whom do you work for?" He raised a fat little index finger. "Think carefully before you lie to me. We know there is another agency above and behind the Central Intelligence Agency. And we know that your Mr. Nero is a front for that other agency. Try to deny it and I will amputate your legs without anesthetic. What is the agency? Who runs it? I want every tiniest detail you have about that agency."

I closed my eyes and sighed a ragged sigh. Gradually the spinning of the room was slowing down and strength was creeping back into my limbs. What I needed desperately was to think, to get my brain back on line.

"OK," I said, "I'll talk."

"No."

I stared at him. "*What?*"

"No, Mr. Mason, when you talk to me, you will be begging to talk. You will be *pleading!*" He turned to Rinpoche. "Come, Rinpoche, let us leave these two youngsters alone to get to know each other. I am sure they have a lot to talk about."

They both laughed out loud and Rinpoche, long and gangly, followed the short, shiny round Montilla across the floor and up the stairs. When the door had closed behind them, I turned to face the simian hulk in front of me. His eyes were small and beady, his jaw was like a slab of granite and his body was a small boulder. I searched for some trace of humanity or thought in his eyes, but there was none. His instructions were to make me suffer, and that was what he planned to do.

He took a couple of steps so he was up close. He cracked his knuckles and balled his fists into two huge rocks. Somewhere in my reeling, aching mind I remembered something about density being more important than weight. His fists looked awful dense. I shifted my gaze to his eyes, and thought that his eyes also looked awful dense. In fact, I thought, we had a potential black hole right there, in the Simian Wonder.

He spread his legs, bent his knees, grabbed his right fist in his left, like he could give it more power like that, and pulled it back like he planned to rip off my head. I knew that if he landed that punch, it was over for me. He wouldn't kill me—he'd been told not to—but he would incapacitate me, and I would be finished.

He went easy. The first dozen blows or so were designed to soften me up without doing too much damage. He started with a few backhanders. I tried to roll with them but that isn't easy when you're chained to a pipe. They were painful and I could taste the blood in my mouth and the ringing in my ears was disorienting me badly. It always pays when you're getting worked over to make it look like you're worse than you really are, but with this animal, I wasn't having to try hard at all. He was killing me, and the pain was real and deep.

He punched me in the belly and almost winded me. He didn't particularly seem to be enjoying himself. His expression was one of indifference, and his attack was methodical. Then he delivered a punch to my floating ribs, and I realized he was moving up from open-handed slaps to punches, and I began to wonder if I was going to make it. I raised my head to look at him and I saw from his stance that the next blow was going to be straight into my face, and I knew that would finish me.

I leaned to the side and spat blood on the floor, then stared him in the eye. I braced myself against the pipe and told him, "Go ahead, you son of a bitch. If you're going to do it, make it count."

He made it count. He balled his fist into a rock, took a step toward me and drove his fist like a pile driver toward my head. It wasn't fast, but it had the force of an express train.

I leaned to my right and the full force of his punch, with his massive weight behind it, smashed into the pipe behind me. The pipe must have been old and rusty because his fist ripped right through the metal and tore the pipe out of the ceiling, and its housing on the floor. He shrieked in agony and I felt the warm blood from his hand and wrist spray over my face. He staggered back a step and I felt the rusty tube collapse behind me. A surge of adrenalin burned in my gut and suddenly I was screaming like a demented daemon. I took a step forward as he staggered back and slammed my right instep into his balls. His face went rigid and tears sprang into his eyes. I was crazy to get my hands on him, but they were still tied behind my back. So I kicked him hard in the side of the knee and as he went down with his bottom lip trembling, I kicked him savagely in the jaw. He fell flat on his face and, for good measure, I stamped my heel into the back of his neck.

Bodily functions controlled by the autonomic system are not always real smart. Your bladder doesn't give a damn if you're in the can, on a bus or at the vicar's tea party: you gotta go, you gotta go. It's the same with shock. If your body decides to go into shock, it doesn't give a damn whether you have a hospital bed to retire to or a hundred crazy jihadists chasing you. You are going to start trembling and get very cold.

In that moment I hurt. It was a kind of universal pain that went from the soles of my feet to the tips of each one of the hairs on my head, and my whole body started trembling uncontrollably. I managed to stagger a couple of steps to where the rusty tube was lying on the floor. I dropped on my knees and, shaking badly, I lined the rope up with the sharp, ragged edge.

It wasn't easy, partly because the pipe kept moving, and partly because the rope was tough, but after about five or ten minutes I managed to cut through it, as well as mangling a good part of the skin on my wrists. By then I was able to stand without my legs going into an Elvis impersonation. I hunkered down beside King Kong and rummaged through his clothes. I didn't find a gun, but I did find a wicked-looking survival knife stuck in his belt. I figured he wouldn't be needing it and slipped it in my waistband. Then I went to look for Dr Montilla and Rinpoche.

TWENTY-TWO

I CLIMBED THE CONCRETE STEPS ONE AT A TIME, working hard to steady my breathing. I am no martial artist, like Gallin. My fighting skills are strictly utilitarian and concern how to end a fight as quickly and efficiently as possible. But I do know enough to understand that rage is not an emotion you want to take into a fight, because it will betray you. So as I climbed each step, I worked at controlling my breathing and getting something like equanimity in my emotions.

The big, wooden door was unlocked, presumably so that Ape Man could leave once he had beaten me in to a vegetative state. I opened the door and stepped out into a corridor with whitewashed walls and a terracotta floor. It ended a couple of feet on my right, and on my left it went for twenty or twenty-five feet to an intersection.

At the intersection I paused and looked right and left. To the right there was a short passage that led to a door. The glass panel in the door told me it was night outside. To the left it led to an illuminated arch beyond which there was a wall tiled halfway up in gaudy tiles with fruit and vegetable motifs on them. I could see also a heavy, rustic table. Even my damaged brain was able to work out I had found the kitchen. A low murmuring with occasional laughter told me I had also found a person watching the TV in that kitchen.

I ambled to the arch and peered in. Can you surprise a Buddhist? Can you surprise a person whose purpose in life is to achieve a permanent state of equanimity? I guess that depends on how far along the path to Nirvana they are. Rinpoche was clearly not that far along the path. He turned from the small, portable TV he was watching and stared at me. He dropped the fork he was holding and it splatted into a plate of scrambled eggs. His eyebrows rose high on his forehead and he gave a small, astonished laugh.

He stood and came around the table. He was nodding and laughing softly. "That is cool. That is so cool." He shrugged and spread his hands. "I not gonna kill you because boss want to talk to you. But I gotta break something."

He didn't wait for an answer. He lunged into a sidekick. Maybe it was the shock, maybe it was exhaustion, but the whole thing played out for me in slow motion. He shifted so his right side was facing me. He did a little, sideways galloping leap and his right foot, encased in a Converse canvas trainer, was moving toward my belly in what must have been a thundering side kick.

I must have moved fast and with real savagery, though it didn't feel like it to me; but Ape Man's hunting knife was in my hand, unsheathed, and I slammed that glinting, silver blade smack into the sole of Rinpoche's foot.

His face twisted, he made ghastly sucking, gasping noises

as he jumped around on his left foot, grabbing at the table, trying not to put his right foot on the floor. I watched the tears flood into his eyes as the crippling pain made his leg quiver and jump. Then shock, exhaustion and pain suddenly erupted into savage rage and I threw my right arm around his neck, gripped my left bicep and clamped my left forearm against the back of his neck. Then I squeezed with all the hatred and rage Zen tells you not to feel, and twisted until I heard the snap.

I let go and he sagged to the floor, with thick blood oozing from his shoe. Buddhists believe that your final, dying thought conditions who you are reincarnated. I figured Rinpoche's dying thought must have been, "Oh, shit!" So, more of the same then.

I opened his jacket and pulled his Glock from under his arm and went in search of Montilla.

Out of the kitchen door there was another corridor at the end of which there was an elaborate Spanish arch that seemed to give onto a living room. I waited, listening, but all I could hear was the yammer and the canned laughter from the TV in the kitchen.

I moved down the passage, flattened myself against the wall and peered through the arch. There was a large room with the same terracotta tiles on the floor. There was an empty fireplace, a couple of leather chairs and sofas and several animal heads—wild boar and deer—mounted on the walls. There were no people. The people were on a terrace outside. Four guys sitting at a table playing cards and drinking tall drinks with plenty of ice. It was a warm night, sultry, and they were chilling while their pal was supposedly destroying me downstairs. I felt the rage begin to smolder again in my belly and fought to control it.

The thought came into my mind that this was not the house where Montilla had drugged my champagne.

I acted without thinking. I crossed the room and stepped out onto the terrace. The three guys at the table looked up at me with very round eyes. The fourth had his back to me. He didn't look round because he had the muzzle of the Glock rammed hard into the back of his neck. I smiled at them.

"You speak English?"

The three whose faces I could see nodded carefully, like if they nodded too fast the gun might go off. I said, "Good. Move too fast, twitch, make me nervous in any way, and I'll blow his brains all over your card game."

They all swallowed at the same time. It was interesting to watch. The one on my left, a heavy-set hairy guy with curly black hair, said, "We no gonna cause no problem. What you want?"

I grinned. "That is the right question. What's your name?"

"Manuel."

"Good, Manuel. You seem smart. Now, tell me this, where is Dr. Montilla?"

The guy opposite me, who had a big moustache and a rabid dog tattooed on his chest, hissed savagely at him, "*No le digas nada, cojones!*"

I raised the Glock ten inches and put a 9mm slug through the tattooed guy's forehead. His head whiplashed and his brains sprayed out over the patio through a hole the size of a grapefruit. For a heartbeat he sat looking astonished, then slumped forward onto his cards. By that time the muzzle of the Glock was back pressing against the back of my guy's neck.

I smiled at Manuel and the guy on my right in turn. "See? Manuel made a good decision, and he is still alive. That guy made a bad decision, and now he is dead. Life is like that sometimes. Now, let's try again. Where is Dr. Montilla?"

I counted to three while they stared first at me and then at each other. Then I shot the guy on my right. That set Manuel waving his hands at me and screaming, "*No! No! No!*" while the guy sitting in front of me with the Glock in his neck started to sob. I shot him in the back of the neck and solved all his problems in less than a second. Then I trained the weapon on Manuel and said, "Have I got your attention yet?"

"*Yesyesyes!*"

"Do you think maybe I am not serious?"

"Nonono! Yesyesyes! I tell you! I tell you!"

"Where-is-Dr.-Montilla?"

He was pointing wildly into the dark, where small lights were glimmering. "In the house. In the big house!"

"This is the guest house?"

"Is the guest house, yes, for Mama, for visit."

"And Montilla is down there?" I pointed.

"In big house, yes. Down there."

I nodded. "OK, thanks. Nothing personal, Manuel. Sorry."

I shot him between the eyes.

There were a couple of trucks parked beside the terrace. I

fished around in the dead guys' pockets and recovered a couple of semi-automatics and a set of keys. A press of a button and a bleep told me my truck was a big old Nissan. I climbed in, fired it up and headed down the track toward the main house.

I didn't turn on the headlamps and I didn't bother stopping. As I approached I could see that at the back of the house he had a swimming pool, a patio and a set of plate-glass doors. They had yellow light filtering through the drapes and, at a rough estimate, I figured they were a little wider than a Nissan truck. So I plowed through the white picket fence, skirted the pool and smashed right through the glass doors and into the living room.

As I swung down from the cab my head was pounding with ill-suppressed rage. There was a smoldering mess of broken wall, shattered glass and mangled furniture, and Montilla was up against the wall, his face twisted with terror and his mouth working silently as he tried to scream; but he was paralyzed by terror and no sound came out.

I picked my way across the rubble toward him. My intention was to put the Glock in his face and make him talk. But my fists had other ideas. I beat his face three times before I got control of myself and dragged him to his knees and thrust my face into his.

"You have one chance to live, Montilla. Just one. As long as I can use you as evidence that there is no oil in Andalusia, you have a chance. But make no mistake, it is taking all my self-control not to blow your damned head off right now. So you had better play ball, Montilla. Believe me, you do not want to make me mad right now."

He managed, "Wh...wh...wh..."

"You know what I want, and you and me are going to go and get it together."

He didn't react. He just knelt there looking at me.

I said, "You are a very stupid man, Montilla. So far your stupidity has cost six men their lives. And before the night is through it may well cost you your life too." He still didn't say anything, so I took a hold of his throat in my hand and snarled, "You need to respond, Montilla, and you need to hand over the evidence that there is no oil under Andalusia, or I am going to do some very bad things to you."

"In my office. It is in my office."

"Now, Montilla. Show me."

He got unsteadily to his feet. I grabbed the back of his collar and thrust the muzzle of the Glock in the small of his back.

"Do something stupid, Montilla, and I will not kill you, but I promise, you'll wish I had."

"No...no..."

He led me out into the hallway, where we crossed to a door opposite. He opened the door and we went in.

It was a large, ample space with a large drawing board in the middle of the floor. The walls were covered in an apparently chaotic mass of photographs, maps and drawings, all representing some aspect of oil wells, oil fields, drilling or refining.

"My whole life," he said, trying to peer at me over his shoulder. "My whole life has been leading up to this..."

"Yeah?" I snarled, "Stop, or you'll break my heart. I want the data-feed boxes which altered the data being received into the main computer from the sonar. I want a hard drive which you installed which received the data bypassing the data-feed, I want your printouts before and after being processed by the Russian computers, which show there is nothing under Granada, Almeria, or any other damn place in Andalusia. I want all that and I want it now, Montilla. Tell you haven't got it and you will be in very serious trouble."

He pointed to a safe over against the far wall. I dragged him over to it and shoved him down on his knees. He scrabbled at the dials with his fingers and after a moment he hauled the heavy, steel door open and dragged out a sports bag which he showed to me with a pathetic, terrified expression on his face. I jerked my head at a coffee table behind him which was situated among a nest of chairs. "On there!"

He lifted the bag onto the table and opened it with trembling hands and pulled out various pieces of computer hardware, showing each one to me in turn.

"The data-feed boxes, the hard drive I installed which bypassed the data-feed," he picked up a sheaf of papers, "printouts, before and after being processed by the Russian computers. They show beyond doubt there is absolutely nothing under the ground here. Please, don't kill me. With this and my testimony you have everything you need. Please, don't kill me." He began to sob and a humiliating dark stain spread across his pants. "Please don't kill me, please!"

I took the bag and closed it, then slung it over my shoulder.

"Get up. You are going to drive me to Gibraltar. I'll be sitting right behind you. You give me a problem and I have nothing to lose. I will shoot you in the spine. Make no mistake."

"I understand."

I was about to gesture him toward the door when a bell jangled. I looked for the sound on his desk and saw it was a cell phone. His face had become drawn and turned a sickly gray color. He swallowed hard. I said, "Answer it."

He shook his head. I raised the Glock and aimed at his forehead. He grabbed the cell with shaking hands and answered. He was shaking so bad he could hardly speak, but he managed, "Si...?"

I mouthed, "Put it on speaker."

He began to sob. A voice I recognized on the phone said, "*José Carlos, que te pasa?*"

He was asking Montilla what was wrong. Montilla's face was collapsing and he was losing control. He began to sob loudly. The voice asked again, more urgently, "*Que te pasa? Estas solo? Háblame!*"

What was wrong, was he alone, and at the end, "Talk to me!"

I went cold from head to foot as all the implications dawned on me. Montilla wailed, with his mouth sagging open, "*No! No, no estoy solo! Huye! Huye!*"

I am not alone, run!

I shot him through the head and he sagged to the floor. I bent and picked up the phone and put it to my ear.

"I recognized your voice," I said. There was only silence. "Did you hear me? I recognized you. You can escape to Russia, but we have people who will track you down."

Then the answer came: "I don't know who you are, friend. But you are a very stupid man if you come up against us. We will hunt you down, we will find you and we will kill you."

"You don't need to hunt me down, pal. You can find me

any day you want to. You just ask for me at the Pentagon, in the State of Virginia. And speaking of stupid, when you threatened me just now, I recorded you. Voice recognition will do the rest."

The line went dead. I dropped the phone in the sports bag and made my way back toward the front door.

TWENTY-THREE

As I entered the hall again I heard the crunch of tires on gravel and the sweep of headlamps glowed through the windows beside the door. I swore profusely and froze. There were voices, a car door slammed, footsteps approached across the terrace. The voices were male, Spanish.

I dropped the bank, went down on one knee and watched the handle of the door rattle. I didn't know how many of them there were. It might be two, it might be four or more. What I wanted here was a silent kill and get the hell out of there. But any hope of that evaporated as I heard a shout from the back of the house. Somebody had seen the carnage the Nissan had caused when it plowed through the glass doors.

I got to my feet, tucked the Glock in my waistband and scrambled for the kitchen and the block of kitchen knives that invariably sits by the cooker in most houses. I was relieved to find this one was no exception and pulled out the large vegetable knife. After that I slipped back into the hall and flattened myself against the wall beside the living-room door. On the other side of it I could hear two men expostulating. I figured they didn't often find Nissan trucks in people's living rooms.

I heard the front door handle rattle and somebody called out. One of the guys in the living room yelled back, "*Voy! Voy!*" *I'm coming, I'm coming.*

I watched the living room door handle turn gently. There was a pause. Then the door opened all the way. A Guardia Civil stepped through, into the hall. At first he was just a dark shape, less than two feet away from me. But as he moved on toward the front door I recognized his green uniform. I waited. He wasn't my target. He took another step and his partner moved through the door behind him. I could just see his shoulder and part of his head. The first guy kept moving, took another two steps, and my target took one more. It was the last step he ever took.

My left hand went over his mouth and with my index finger I sealed his nose. Before he could make a noise, I drove the point of the kitchen knife into the side of his neck, cutting through his carotid artery and his jugular. Then I punched forward hard, slicing right through his windpipe. The blood sprayed like a hose under pressure all over his pal's back as he jerked and quivered like crazy. I let him go and he dropped to the floor. His partner was turning, his eyes wide and his mouth open.

I stepped forward fast, gripped the barrel of his automatic in my left hand and levered down savagely as I drove the blade of the kitchen knife had through his throat. I felt it split the vertebrae at the back of his neck and he dropped straight to the floor. As he did so I heard a loud crack out front and knew the remaining two had shot out the lock. I had to act fast. I ran two steps, dropped to the floor as the door opened and put six shots blind into the two hulking shadows framed in the doorway. They both went down screaming. I scrambled to my feet, ran and grabbed the sports bag, jumped over the dying men and out onto the veranda.

I could have run. I should have run. I could have taken their Range Rover and got the hell out of there. But I didn't know how many of them there were, if they were all dead or if there were enough of them left to come after me. And that was something I really didn't need. So I made a run for the back of the house and sure enough, as I flattened myself against the wall, I saw the two remaining *Guardia,* just as they were peering in through the wrecked glass doors.

I don't often miss a shot, but I was exhausted and probably still in shock. I aimed, held my breath and squeezed, but as I did so my target stepped into the house and his partner stepped into my line of fire. Shit happens. The bullet went in through his right side and must have punched a hole right through his heart. He staggered and dropped.

I stepped forward intending to take down the first guy, but in that moment he stepped back out, saw me and leveled his automatic. He fired as I dropped and emptied my magazine in his direction. He fell, but he fell into the house and I didn't know how badly hurt he was.

I decided not to compound my mistake by going after him, jumped to my feet and ran. I made Montilla's Mercedes as the wounded cop hobbled around the veranda. He squeezed off two shots that went wide and I reversed like crazy toward the road. The last I saw of him he was talking into a radio. That was exactly what I had wanted to avoid. As I hit the gas, I was swearing profanities that hadn't been invented yet.

I plowed through the gate in reverse. Made the brakes scream as I spun the wheel, slammed in first, surged forward in a spray of gravel and dirt, second, third and fourth, burning rubber toward the blacktop.

All the while I was shouting at myself in my mind: *What's your plan? God damn it! What's your plan? What the hell do you do now?*

But I knew. It was simple. There was only one possible plan. Gibraltar was impossible. The wounded cop had got on his radio, so not only would the border be crawling with cops and soldiers all looking for me and my sports bag, I had not heard from Gallin, which meant there was a good chance they had been stopped and arrested. I had to get the evidence in my sports bag to an American embassy, fast. The only way to do that was to head north and cross the front line. The assault from Spain had not started yet, with just a little luck I might make the border before it started.

Head north and try to get across the lines into Spain. That was the plan. Head north.

To paraphrase the old Yiddish proverb, men make plans so that the gods can laugh. The gods may well have been laughing, but I sure as hell wasn't. The Merc gripped the road like it had claws on its wheels. I was driving like I was demented, screaming around the mountain roads, cutting the corners on the hairpins, shaving the edges, inches from the black ravines. trusting fate destiny karma or old One-Eye

Odin himself that I would not meet a vehicle coming head-on.

I met no traffic, but pretty soon I began to hear a crazy screaming overhead. And as I slowed to peer out the window I saw what it was. They were fighter-bombers, whether they were Andalusian or Spanish I couldn't tell, howling toward Almeria. It had started.

Soon afterwards the choppers started, circling overhead, playing their searchlights over the roads and the woodlands below. I knew they were hunting for me, and I knew it was just a matter of time before they found me.

I switched off the headlamps. As long as I was in the mountains, in the dark, I had a chance. But even as I thought that I knew that If I was going to head north through the mountains I had to go through the Zafaraya Pass, and that meant two things. First it meant taking the A-402 and crossing the Valley of La Viñuela. The A-402 was a major road and for about ten miles I would be totally exposed, especially with the total absence of anything but military traffic at the moment.

It also meant getting through the Zafaraya Pass. It was not strategically vital, but it was strategically important because it gave access from the north to Malaga, which was a vital port. It would be heavily guarded, and getting around the roadblock at the pass would mean ditching the Mercedes and doing some serious mountain climbing. The pass was wild, high and steep.

I had no idea how I was going to do it, and in the end I decided all I could do was make it up as I went along, one objective at a time.

My first objective was getting through the Valley of the

Viñuela without get shot to pieces by a chopper. That was fine as far as it went, but by the time I started my descent toward the Valley and the A-402, I still had no damned idea what I was going to do. And to make matters more interesting, not only were there fighter-bombers streaking over head, and choppers making grid-pattern searches of the area, now the northern horizon was lighting up like there was an electric storm going on. Two got you twenty that as the fleet was steaming in from Majorca, a major artillery push had started in the northeast, in Extremadura, driving down the E-803, and another from Albacete, in Castille, pushing down the Guadalquivir Valley, driving through Jaen and Cordoba, forming a pincer movement closing on Seville, the capital.

The building chaos could work for me or against me. Once I reached the bottom of the winding mountain road I would lose my cover. I'd be exposed for maybe ten miles in the open ranges before I reached the mountains again and started to climb toward the pass. But if the fledgling Republic of Andalusia was being pounded from the north, the east and possibly even the south, they might just have too much on their hands to search for a single vehicle.

I knew it was wishful thinking, because that single vehicle was transporting the evidence that could kill the bid for independence overnight, and it was being transported in what was probably the only luxury Mercedes Benz on the road that night.

Then two things happened simultaneously. I saw a checkpoint up ahead, half a mile away with a Defender parked beside it, and I had a flash of inspiration.

Coming down the winding mountain road I had been hitting the gas in third and fourth, moving fast but controlling the engine. Now, on the final straight, I switched the headlamps onto full beam, opened the windows, shifted to fifth and sixth and floored the pedal. The powerful car surged and I watched the needle climb to a hundred and eighty kilometers per hour and keep climbing. Ahead of me there were a couple of soldiers waving their arms like crazy. For an insane moment they took aim with their rifles, but I was moving at one hundred and sixty-five feet per second—that's fifty-five yards every time you said, "And one." They chickened and scattered as the Merc hit the barrier, I slammed on the brakes and spun the wheel, scattering wood, gravel and terrified guards.

By the time the car came to a halt its beams were glaring on the two huddled soldiers who were shielding their eyes with their arms. I stepped out of the Mercedes and shot them dead where they crouched. I didn't like doing it. In any other situation they would probably have been nice college kids you'd be happy to have a beer with. But right then they would have shot me dead without hesitation. Life sucks, but that's not news.

I killed the lights on the Merc and drove it into the ditch, under the cover of some almond trees. Overhead a chopper thundered across the sky, a few hundred feet up, obscuring the stars and playing a spotlight over the almond and olive groves. They knew, like I did, that sooner or later I was going to have to break cover and move into that valley. But they'd be looking for a black Mercedes, and I'd be driving a military Land Rover.

I fished the keys out of one of the soldier's pocket, grabbed their two HK G36 assault rifles, climbed into the cab, slammed the door and drove fast the last few hundred yards down to the bottom of the valley. There I found a T-junction and fishtailed onto the A-402, then floored the pedal. It didn't take long for one of the choppers to notice me. He came in low and buzzed me twice. I made like he wasn't there, and pretty soon I guess he decided I wasn't a black Mercedes Benz and he went away, back into the mountains.

After five minutes I came to a convoy of trucks hurtling south toward the coast. Some general somewhere had decided the Mediterranean coastal defenses needed shoring up, so maybe the Russian and Algerian support hadn't been as effective as they'd hoped. Or maybe they were just being careful. I thundered past them and a couple of minutes after that I was climbing up into the mountains again, toward the Zafaraya Pass.

The higher I went the tighter the hairpin bends became, and the steeper the mountainsides. I was forced to slow down to no more than fifty miles per hour, if I wanted to make it to the front lines.

By the time I sighted the pass, about half a mile up ahead, the mountains rising above the road were near vertical. I had no idea how many guards I was going to find at the checkpoint. The optimist in me told me they'd be deploying as many men as they possibly could to the fronts. The realist in my told me that's not how armies work. War has very little to do with logic.

I checked the magazines of the various weapons I'd collected, and approached the checkpoint at a steady speed. Pretty soon a guy in uniform emerged from a red and white hut and started waving a flashlight at me. I slowed. Two more guys emerged from the hut. They were carrying weapons but they didn't look like they were about to shoot anybody. I guess if I had been coming from the north it might have been different. But I was coming from the inside, and I wasn't a crazy, speeding black Mercedes, so I was not an immediate threat.

The two guys with the rifles stayed at the barrier while the guy with the flashlight signaled me to come closer. I did, at a crawl. Behind the three men at the barrier, I now saw two more guards at the door of the hut. One was holding a cup in both hands and sipping from it. Five men. I wondered if that was the total. It seemed right, but who knew?

I let the truck crawl forward while I picked up the first of the Heckler and Koch rifles. I double-tapped the guy with the flashlight and shattered my windshield in the process. As he went down I sprayed the two guys with rifles behind the barrier. For a moment I was blinded by the shattered windshield and they returned fire. But their first target was my headlamps, which were blinding them. And by the time they got around to me, they were already dead.

I hit the gas. And smashed through the barrier. I'd noticed the two uniforms at the hut had dashed inside, probably to fetch their weapons. I didn't let them do that. I slammed on the brakes and, snatching up the other Heckler, I sprayed the cabin from halfway down to the floor. When I was done, I dropped the rifle on the blacktop, walked up to the hut and opened the door. There were three guys in there, not two, and they were all dead.

My Land Rover was bleeding steam from several bullet holes in the radiator. So I searched the dead soldiers for another set of keys and took a Spanish Santana Anibal, which is basically a Land Rover Defender with a different name. I clambered in, fired her up and hurtled through the small, sleepy town of Zafaraya, where all the windows were closed and dark, hiding the terrified, peering eyes of the villagers, wondering how much longer I could keep going before they caught me.

The answer wasn't long in coming.

TWENTY-FOUR

SOMEONE IN THE VILLAGE MUST HAVE MADE THE call. Because it was only fifteen minutes later that I heard the thunder of the choppers closing in behind me. I was doing nearly eighty on the mountain roads. It was a miracle I hadn't killed myself already. But when I heard the choppers I hit the gas and looked in my wing mirror. Not for the first time that night I swore violently. There were two Russian Mil Mi 24P gunships on my tail with their spots glaring, and that meant exactly one thing. I was already dead.

I was on a straight road running which ran through a flat highland. The truck was no match for the choppers even on a winding road, but in a straight line it was game over. Pretty soon they had drawn level. One of them settled on my right and the other took up a position in front of me. I knew the next thing would be to riddle me and the truck with heavy machine-gun fire. So I figured I had nothing to lose. I swung the wheel left and careened into the field on my left, bounding and skidding among the olive trees.

I had no idea how far I'd get. I knew for a certainty that I was going to die. But I also knew I was not ready to go down yet. So I bounced and hurtled across the dirt, skidding and sliding among the trees, occasionally smashing and scraping the sides against the ancient trunks, spraying dirt wide into the night air, and all over the windshield.

The gunships were behind me now, rising above the trees. I swung left and right, missing the trees. The guns on the chopper on my left opened up and a fountain of dirt exploded beside me, spraying across my windshield and leaving me blind.

I hit the windshield wiper which made it worse and ended up shooting out the windshield. I sideswiped one tree on my left, bounced and hit another on my right. The shattered windshield fell away behind me as I watched the searchlights closing in on me. I heard the violent crackle of machine guns and a second later heavy slugs tore through the rear of the truck. I skidded sideways and just before I started to roll I grabbed the sports bag, kicked open the door and jumped. Somehow, by some miracle, I wasn't killed.

Rocks, stones and trees made a pretty good job of tearing me apart, but after five or six seconds that felt a hell of a lot longer, the old truck hit the bottom of the slope and exploded into flames, as I staggered to my feet and ran, limping, for the darkness.

It was a forlorn hope. It might have been a rock, a stone or the root of an olive tree. Or it might have been sheer exhaustion. I tripped and fell flat on my face. I lay a few seconds gasping with long shards of pain piercing my back and chest. Finally I looked up and behind me and struggled to my feet.

I was standing in the full glow of the spotlights. From one of the choppers I saw ropes unfurl and soldiers begin to descend. I backed up a few steps, then turned and ran. Though more than running it was plowing painfully and slowly through the loose, dry earth. My back and chest were screaming with pain from the crash, and from the pounding they had taken before. My legs were trembling and they muscles were seizing up with every step. I kept telling myself if I could make it over the next hill, disappear into the undergrowth and the wilderness, I might just be able to make it to the front line. I was dragging my legs forward, not running but hobbling, and I was aware that I was stumbling in the unwavering light of a spot. I was moving so slowly that, whatever I did, there was no way I could shake it. I was not so much a sitting duck, as a stumbling duck, waiting to be shot.

Then I was at a bank, where the field fell away into darkness. Over the thud of the rotors I could hear men shouting behind me. They were telling me to stop or they would shoot. I fell. I let myself fall into the void. For a moment there was stillness and darkness and quiet rest. But it was less than a second and then I hit dirt and stones and rocks, and pain again. I tumbled and rolled, hit trees and rocks and finally came to a halt and lay staring up at the black sky, where cruel, indifferent specks of ice looked back at me and just didn't care.

My throat was raw with panting and gasping for air. I didn't want to run anymore. I knew I was about to die and I had always promised myself I would not die fleeing. I was going to turn and face them, and die fighting. I saw myself get to my feet and start to climb the hill, realized I was dreaming and forced myself up onto one elbow. I watched the glow of the spots illuminate the hilltop. The roar and thud of the rotors filled the air and I watched the black silhouettes of the olive trees bow and dance in the downdraft. I roared out loud as I forced myself onto one knee and the downdraft started to batter my face, tearing at my hair as the dust and dirt were whipped up into a storm around me.

Some madness inside me told me this gave me an advantage, as they would not see me as I crept up on them and killed them, one by one.

I staggered a couple of feeble steps back the way I had come. The searching circles of the spots were fifty or a hundred yards away from me. Ahead, at the top of the hill I could see the silhouettes of maybe six or eight soldiers advancing toward the illuminated areas as the spots swept this way and that.

I was about to bend and grab a rock—that would be my weapon—but something, an indefinable sensation, made me turn and look behind me. At the crest of that slope, almost invisible, there was a silhouette. It was kneeling, holding something to its face, like some kind of scope. It was immobile, unreal, like a dream.

Then there was a column of fire that streaked across the dark sky and made me gasp. A second later there was another and suddenly the helicopters were enveloped in brilliant flames that rained down onto the trees and the soldiers as the huge fuel tanks erupted and rained down burning death. I was blinded by the light from the fireballs as the heat washed over me.

Then something gripped my arm. I turned, unalarmed,

ready to die, and saw Gallin frowning at me. I smiled at her. "I must be dead," I told her. "Are you dead too?"

"Not yet, Mason, but I'm working on it. Come on, let's get out of here."

Behind her I saw two large men running down the hill. One of them shouted in a cheerful, cockney voice, "Come on darlin', Jimmy wants to get home and have his tea!"

That was where I blacked out.

———

IT WAS the kind of bizarre image that would make you think either you were dead and in some bizarre afterlife imagined by Salvador Dali, or turning gently psychotic and hallucinating. Nero was sitting beside a large turquoise swimming pool with a vast, Mediterranean sky behind him, on a cliff high above the sea. He was wearing white slacks, a cream shirt and very black sunglasses, and watching me. We were at a villa in Gibraltar.

"The most bizarre thing of all," I told him, "was that you actually bothered to pack those clothes, knowing you were coming to a war zone."

He turned from me to Gallin, who was sitting by my side holding a long gin and tonic.

"I have told your father that I consider facetious men to be fundamentally immature and a bad match for any sensible woman."

She smiled politely. "I am sure he agreed with you."

"He did. He is an intelligent man and not at all facetious."

"Everything hurts," I told him, wincing as I shifted my

bruised body from a painful position to a less painful one. "Can't you be kind to me, just for today?"

If he displayed an expression it was concealed by his huge sunglasses.

"A great deal has happened while you were asleep," he said, as though answering a question. "I am surprised you didn't stay awake to hear the news."

I narrowed my eyes. I would have sworn I saw the glimmer of a smile at the corner of his mouth, but then reassured myself it was my still fragile psyche playing tricks on me.

"Like what?" I asked.

"The evidence you collected was flown to the American embassy in Paris, where an emergency meeting of NATO heads of state and top brass was convened. The Russian ambassador was summoned and in the small hours of the morning an emergency summit was held with the president of the United States, the top brass of NATO and the heads of state of the major contributing nations."

I grinned at Gallin in a way I hoped was both dashingly heroic but also endearingly vulnerable. "I made all that happen?" I said.

To my surprise her expression was sympathetic. Nero ignored me.

"At five o'clock this morning, Greenwich Mean Time, Russia and Iran both formally withdrew their support for an independent Andalusia, the Andalusian defense collapsed and Spanish troops marched into Seville, where Benjamin Musa was arrested. He is now in jail awaiting arraignment."

"All that while I was asleep?"

"Indeed."

"What about Torreras, the Minister for Oil?"

"He and a number of others have been arrested. The CIA are collaborating with Spanish officials in interrogating and debriefing various officials who have been arrested. Some will face trial, others will not, particularly if they are helpful in clarifying how all this was able to happen."

"By which you mean provide information on Russian counterintelligence and Russian-Iranian relations. What about Anna Garcia?"

"She has been very helpful in informing us about Mr. Torreras. She has not been arrested."

"Good."

"Do you feel up to some food? You look appallingly weak. I am surprised you survived."

"Maybe some chicken soup and a couple of large whiskeys. Tell me something." I turned to Gallin. "Did I dream it, or were you with British troops when you found me?"

"Some friends of mine from the Special Air Service, on unofficial duty observing the progress of the Spanish offensive."

"How did you know where I was?"

"British GCHQ was hacking into Spanish communications via Gibraltar. When the helicopters located you, we moved in."

I nodded. "When you didn't call I thought you'd both been arrested. So what happened to Colonel Alexandrina Vitsin?"

Gallin looked away and Nero grunted. He answered, "Part of the tradeoff. I was against it, but the president insisted. In his view an immediate settlement was essential, so I was overridden. She was handed back and the Russians withdrew. She was sworn to kill me, and she knows ODIN exists, even if she is not fully aware of its form and function. She knows we are *there!*"

I sighed. "Speaking of presidents. Just before I killed Dr. Montilla, he received a phone call. I don't know what the call was about, because the caller pretty quickly realized something was wrong with Montilla and started asking him if he was OK and if he was alone. Montilla told him he was not alone, and to escape. I recognized the voice."

Nero was watching me carefully. "Who was it?" he asked.

"It was the Spanish president, Alvaro Romero."

He went very still, then heaved a huge sigh. "I had imagined as much." He glanced at Gallin. "I told your father. If this declaration of independence, and the ensuing civil war, were engineered by the Russians, then it was essential for Andalusia to have an intransigent Spanish leader to oppose them. Jesus Sanchez, for all his right-wing credentials, was at heart a negotiator. He would have prevaricated and attempted to find a peaceful solution, aware, as any intelligent man would have been, of the possible repercussions of an armed conflict in the heart of the European Union. When he died my suspicions were aroused and I suspected straight away that Romero was Russia's man. His inflammatory oratory and his refusal to contemplate any solution other than an invasion confirmed it."

Gallin shook her head. "So Russia was playing both sides? The Spanish and the Andalusian leaders were both Russian puppets?"

Nero nodded. "I am afraid so. And this whole thing was

engineered by Colonel Alexandrina Vitsin, who has been allowed to walk free, back to her den in Moscow."

I was frowning, trying to stay alert but succumbing to sleepiness and exhaustion.

"So what about Alvaro Romero? Does he walk too?"

Nero removed his huge, black sunglasses and frowned at me. "Your evidence is far too thin, Alex, to substantiate such a serious allegation. Sometimes the bad guy gets away. Unless," he said, as he slipped his shades back on, "he happens to be struck by a Cobra or something."

It struck me as a strange thing to say, but I was too tired to mention it and I drifted into sweet, restful, mending sleep. The last thing I remember is Nero telling Gallin he was going to go and get some lunch. Then there was the soft lapping of the pool and, it may have been a dream, but I'd swear she gave me a kiss.

I guess I'll never know.

EPILOGUE

Some six hundred and twenty miles to the northeast Alvaro Romero trotted down the steps of the parliament. His expression was one of triumph and joy, and he waved to the gathered crowd who cheered and chanted his name.

But inwardly what he felt was anxiety. He could not eradicate the voice from his head, the voice that told him coldly, cruelly, "I recognized your voice. Did you hear me? I recognized you...we have people who will track you down."

He told himself they needed him. After the negotiations with Russia they needed him. Spain looked to him as a symbol of strength and unity. He was the rebirth of a credible right wing, and he was the rebirth of Spain, a strong Spain the people could believe in.

He noticed a tiny flash of light from across the square in the Calle de San Agustin. It was a fraction of a second, but it was a timeless moment because in that instant he knew he was about to die.

The bullet smacked into his forehead and exploded out the back of his head. And President Alvaro Romero, the courageous savior of a united Spain, entered the Spanish history books as that rarest of things, a true national hero.

The assassin walked quietly away, having left the weapon in a dumpster, along with his latex gloves. As he walked he called a secure number outside New York.

"Done," he said simply, and hung up. Later he would burn the phone and dispose of it. He reflected briefly on his boss's words when he had been given the assignment. He had asked, "Wouldn't it make sense to keep him in power? He's a hero, he's popular, and with the information we have on him, we'd own him."

His boss had laughed and shaken his head, and told him, "You're right up to a point, but we let them get overconfident, we let them think we were getting weak. That can't happen. They have to hear the message. The message has to go out loud and clear. Don't fuck with DC."

Don't miss BROTHERHOOD OF THE GOAT. The riveting sequel in the Alex Mason Thriller series.

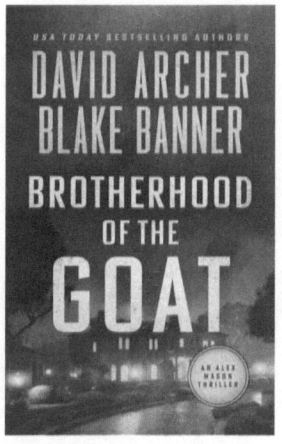

Scan the QR code below to purchase BROTHERHOOD OF THE GOAT

Or go to: righthouse.com/brotherhood-of-the-goat

NOTE: flip to the very end to read an exclusive sneak peak...

DON'T MISS ANYTHING!

If you want to stay up to date on all new releases in this series, with these authors, or with any of our new deals, you can do so by joining our newsletters below.

In addition, you will immediately gain access to our entire *Right House VIP Library,* which currently includes *ORIGINS*—a full length prequel novel to *ODIN.*

righthouse.com/email

(Easy to unsubscribe. No spam. Ever.)

ALSO BY DAVID ARCHER

Up to date books can be found at:
www.righthouse.com/david-archer

ROGUE THRILLERS
Gates of Hell (Book 1)
Hell's Fury (Book 2)

JACOB HUNTER THRILLERS
The Kyiv File (Book 1)
The Bogota File (Book 2)

PETER BLACK THRILLERS
Burden of the Assassin (Book 1)
The Man Without A Face (Book 2)
Unpunished Deeds (Book 3)
Hunter Killer (Book 4)
Silent Shadows (Book 5)
The Last Run (Book 6)
Dark Corners (Book 7)
Ghost Operative (Book 8)

ALEX MASON THRILLERS
Odin (Book 1)
Ice Cold Spy (Book 2)
Mason's Law (Book 3)
Assets and Liabilities (Book 4)
Russian Roulette (Book 5)

Executive Order (Book 6)
Dead Man Talking (Book 7)
All The King's Men (Book 8)
Flashpoint (Book 9)
Brotherhood of the Goat (Book 10)
Dead Hot (Book 11)
Blood on Megiddo (Book 12)
Son of Hell (Book 13)

NOAH WOLF THRILLERS
Code Name Camelot (Book 1)
Lone Wolf (Book 2)
In Sheep's Clothing (Book 3)
Hit for Hire (Book 4)
The Wolf's Bite (Book 5)
Black Sheep (Book 6)
Balance of Power (Book 7)
Time to Hunt (Book 8)
Red Square (Book 9)
Highest Order (Book 10)
Edge of Anarchy (Book 11)
Unknown Evil (Book 12)
Black Harvest (Book 13)
World Order (Book 14)
Caged Animal (Book 15)
Deep Allegiance (Book 16)
Pack Leader (Book 17)
High Treason (Book 18)
A Wolf Among Men (Book 19)
Rogue Intelligence (Book 20)
Alpha (Book 21)

Rogue Wolf (Book 22)
Shadows of Allegiance (Book 23)
In the Grip of Darkness (Book 24)

SAM PRICHARD MYSTERIES
The Grave Man (Book 1)
Death Sung Softly (Book 2)
Love and War (Book 3)
Framed (Book 4)
The Kill List (Book 5)
Drifter: Part One (Book 6)
Drifter: Part Two (Book 7)
Drifter: Part Three (Book 8)
The Last Song (Book 9)
Ghost (Book 10)
Hidden Agenda (Book 11)

SAM AND INDIE MYSTERIES
Aces and Eights (Book 1)
Fact or Fiction (Book 2)
Close to Home (Book 3)
Brave New World (Book 4)
Innocent Conspiracy (Book 5)
Unfinished Business (Book 6)
Live Bait (Book 7)
Alter Ego (Book 8)
More Than It Seems (Book 9)
Moving On (Book 10)
Worst Nightmare (Book 11)
Chasing Ghosts (Book 12)
Serial Superstition (Book 13)

CHANCE REDDICK THRILLERS
Innocent Injustice (Book 1)
Angel of Justice (Book 2)
High Stakes Hunting (Book 3)
Personal Asset (Book 4)

CASSIE MCGRAW MYSTERIES
What Lies Beneath (Book 1)
Can't Fight Fate (Book 2)
One Last Game (Book 3)
Never Really Gone (Book 4)

ALSO BY BLAKE BANNER

Up to date books can be found at:
www.righthouse.com/blake-banner

ROGUE THRILLERS
Gates of Hell (Book 1)
Hell's Fury (Book 2)

ALEX MASON THRILLERS
Odin (Book 1)
Ice Cold Spy (Book 2)
Mason's Law (Book 3)
Assets and Liabilities (Book 4)
Russian Roulette (Book 5)
Executive Order (Book 6)
Dead Man Talking (Book 7)
All The King's Men (Book 8)
Flashpoint (Book 9)
Brotherhood of the Goat (Book 10)
Dead Hot (Book 11)
Blood on Megiddo (Book 12)
Son of Hell (Book 13)

HARRY BAUER THRILLER SERIES
Dead of Night (Book 1)
Dying Breath (Book 2)
The Einstaat Brief (Book 3)

Quantum Kill (Book 4)

Immortal Hate (Book 5)

The Silent Blade (Book 6)

LA: Wild Justice (Book 7)

Breath of Hell (Book 8)

Invisible Evil (Book 9)

The Shadow of Ukupacha (Book 10)

Sweet Razor Cut (Book 11)

Blood of the Innocent (Book 12)

Blood on Balthazar (Book 13)

Simple Kill (Book 14)

Riding The Devil (Book 15)

The Unavenged (Book 16)

The Devil's Vengeance (Book 17)

Bloody Retribution (Book 18)

Rogue Kill (Book 19)

Blood for Blood (Book 20)

DEAD COLD MYSTERY SERIES

An Ace and a Pair (Book 1)

Two Bare Arms (Book 2)

Garden of the Damned (Book 3)

Let Us Prey (Book 4)

The Sins of the Father (Book 5)

Strange and Sinister Path (Book 6)

The Heart to Kill (Book 7)

Unnatural Murder (Book 8)

Fire from Heaven (Book 9)

To Kill Upon A Kiss (Book 10)

Murder Most Scottish (Book 11)

The Butcher of Whitechapel (Book 12)
Little Dead Riding Hood (Book 13)
Trick or Treat (Book 14)
Blood Into Wine (Book 15)
Jack In The Box (Book 16)
The Fall Moon (Book 17)
Blood In Babylon (Book 18)
Death In Dexter (Book 19)
Mustang Sally (Book 20)
A Christmas Killing (Book 21)
Mommy's Little Killer (Book 22)
Bleed Out (Book 23)
Dead and Buried (Book 24)
In Hot Blood (Book 25)
Fallen Angels (Book 26)
Knife Edge (Book 27)
Along Came A Spider (Book 28)
Cold Blood (Book 29)
Curtain Call (Book 30)

THE OMEGA SERIES
Dawn of the Hunter (Book 1)
Double Edged Blade (Book 2)
The Storm (Book 3)
The Hand of War (Book 4)
A Harvest of Blood (Book 5)
To Rule in Hell (Book 6)
Kill: One (Book 7)
Powder Burn (Book 8)
Kill: Two (Book 9)
Unleashed (Book 10)

ABOUT US

Right House is an independent publisher created by authors for readers. We specialize in Action, Thriller, Mystery, and Crime novels.

If you enjoyed this novel, then there is a good chance you will like what else we have to offer! Please stay up to date by using any of the links below.

Join our mailing lists to stay up to date -->
righthouse.com/email
Visit our website --> righthouse.com
Contact us --> contact@righthouse.com

 facebook.com/righthousebooks
x.com/righthousebooks
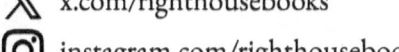 instagram.com/righthousebooks

EXCLUSIVE SNEAK PEAK OF...

BROTHERHOOD OF THE GOAT

PROLOGUE

FRAZER BENSON THOUGHT HE WAS IMMORTAL. Especially when he took his red capsule. When he was drunk, he was sure he was immortal. Right now, he was drunk. He had been at Jack Magnuson's eighty-sixth birthday party, he had taken two of the reds, and he had drunk enough to float the fleet.

He was in his Bentley Continental convertible cruising up Sunset Boulevard through Holmby Hills, remembering the press of glittering people. The people sparkled more than the diamonds they were wearing. There every goddamned star in Hollywood there. You *had* to be there. If you weren't there, pal, you were nobody. And *he* had been there. He laughed out loud to the sky. He, Frazer Benson, had been there. Not only had he been there, he had been invited personally by Jack Magnuson himself. The man who was going to be honored at the next Oscars as the greatest cinema actor of the twentieth and the twenty-first centuries.

That was the man who had invited him to his eighty-sixth birthday party.

He came to the big intersection with Benedict Canyon Drive. The lights were red for him, but he cut across anyway into Hartford Way. He heard a couple of horns behind him, gave them the finger, and laughed.

"*Screw you!*" he screamed. "*I got invited to Jack Magnuson's birthday party! Losers!*"

He chuckled. He knew it was childish, but he didn't give a damn. He was a god.

He pulled up at his gate. He knew there was nobody at home. His wife was at her mother's. He thought about getting a couple of hookers, but he was tired. It was four a.m., and there was the risk his wife would come back before they'd left. The gate rolled open, and he rolled in. Then it rolled closed behind him with a big clang.

He didn't bother putting the car in the garage. Suddenly he was tired and just wanted a nightcap and bed. He climbed from his car and walked, a little unsteadily, across the lawn to the big oak front door flanked by the marble columns he had imported personally from Persia. He liked to think of it as Persia when he thought about his columns. They had once belonged to a Persian king, after all. He chuckled as he fit his key into the lock. Persia made carpets and marble columns. Iran was a place you bombed.

He noticed absently that there was a dim light in his drawing-room window. That was odd because his wife was not home. His wife called it the living room, but his mother had taught him that common people live in their living rooms, whereas people with class withdraw to the drawing room. He let himself in. The door closed behind him with a heavy clunk. He hung up his coat and his scarf and entered the drawing room, undoing his bowtie and telling himself he was definitely not common.

He had reached the credenza and was pouring himself a twenty-one-year-old Bushmills single malt when he became aware, by some sixth sense, that somebody was sitting watching him from the couch by the window, under the standard lamp. He turned.

He could see the legs, the very shiny black shoes, and the slender white hands, but the face and the body were in shadow.

"Who the hell—"

"You weren't expecting me."

The voice was disembodied, emerging from the dark. It wasn't a question. It was more like an observation. The voice was quiet, almost melodious. Frazer frowned.

"You..."

"Tom called me."

"Tom?"

"He said you were talking to Melanie Westwood."

"Yeah." Frazer pointed to the silver tray of decanters. "You want a drink?"

"No. She is a wonderful actress. The best, in my book. She and Magnuson dominated the twentieth century. Real artists. Shame they only made two movies together." Frazer nodded, gaping slightly, half listening but mainly wondering what the hell was going on. The voice said, "She refused to work with him, you know. He's a genius, but he's an animal, a Hell's Angel turned movie star. That's why Humberto loves him." A quiet laugh. "He was all over her, making sexual advances, groping her. She's a lady. An elegant

woman." A pause. "But magnetic, electrifying, sensual—"
He paused again, giving meaning to his next words. "The kind of woman any man would want to impress."

Frazer lowered himself into a chair. "Uh, Lou, you know it's always a pleasure to see you guys—"

"No."

"Huh...?" Frazer's eyes went wide and he smiled.

"It is not always a pleasure to see us, Frazer. Sometimes we torture people."

He laughed. "You *what?*"

There was a subtle shift in the voice. It was still soft, still quiet, but now there was a relentless, unforgiving hardness to it. "We explain very clearly at the beginning that there are absolute red lines. Stay within the lines and the benefits can be unlimited, but you do not cross the lines."

"Sure, but—"

"You don't cross the lines, Frazer. If you cross the lines, just as the benefits of obedience are potentially unlimited, so the punishment for crossing the lines can be unlimited. Sometimes we torture people."

The smile had melted from Frazer's face like warm wax. He had gone pale, and there was a hot pellet of fear in his belly that made him want to vomit.

"Listen, but I didn't—"

"Tom told us what you did and what you didn't do. He heard your conversation and he felt the need to intervene. I am going to ask you. Frazer. What would have happened, what would you have told Melanie, if he had not butted into your conversation?"

"No, nothing. I just said—"

"I know what you said, Frazer. Tom told me."

"But it was nothing. I—"

"It wasn't nothing, Frazer. It was a red line, and you crossed it."

A soft noise behind him made him turn. There were two men. They both wore expensive dark gray suits. They both had black bags over their heads. Absurdly he wondered how they could see. Lou laughed out loud.

"Relax, Frazer! Come on! We're family! We are not going to hurt you. I just wanted to scare you a bit. Consider this a first warning. If it happens again, things will be a lot more serious."

Frazer laughed once, too loud, then relaxed into his chair with his heart pounding.

"You guys. If what you wanted was to scare me, you sure succeeded!"

It was as he said "succeeded" that he felt the sharp bee sting in his arm. He turned, frowning, and saw that it was not a bee, but a syringe. The needle had penetrated his jacket sleeve and his shirt and plunged deep into his arm. His arm throbbed. He tried to move it, but the guy with the black cloth bag on his head was holding down his wrist. On the other side, the other guy was doing the same. He turned to Lou. Lou stood and came out of the shadows. His long, thin, pale face was smiling. He came and hunkered down in front of Frazer, one long, thin hand on each knee.

"You remember I said we were not going to hurt you?"

Frazer tried to nod, but the impulse never reached his muscles.

"It's a distillation of curare. It paralyzes your muscles but does not rob you of feeling. You can still feel the whole, rich range of sensations." His smile broadened. It seemed to

Frazer to be full of sharp, terrifying angles, his mouth like an arrow tip pointing down, his nose like a dagger, his eyes like two blades. "But I told you, didn't I, that we would not hurt you." He drew his face so close to Fraser's that their noses were touching, and his slit eyes penetrated into Frazer's, his breath stinking in Frazer's nose. His voice, when it came, was a vicious rasp. "*Well, I lied, Frazer, because we are going to hurt you a lot!*"

CHAPTER 1

NERO PUT A GRAPE IN HIS MOUTH AND CHEWED, then sipped his Armagnac, a *Bas Armagnac de Gaube*, from the *appellation contrôlée Corderoy du Tiers*.

"Really," he said, doing a lot of vaguely unpleasant stuff with his mouth, "really very good. Rare. Hard to get hold of. Extremely good."

I watched him and waited with a smile that never made it past my nose. When he had finally smacked his lips and reached for another grape, I spoke.

"Sir, when somebody, even an actress, even a great actress and a Hollywood star, reports a murder, that is an FBI matter. That's not our jurisdiction."

He froze halfway through a chew and arched an eyebrow at me. I cleared my throat. "Obviously you know that. So I am guessing there must be some good reason why you want me to travel to Los Angeles and talk to Melanie Westwood."

He finished his chew. "That would not be an unreasonable assumption, Alex." He sipped his Armagnac and leaned back in his chair while he savored it. "First, we have no juris-dictional limits. Second, Miss Westwood approached the Federal Bureau of Investigation a week ago, a few days after hearing of the death of Frazer Benson. Mr. Benson was an acquaintance of hers. They had many friends and acquain-tances in common. I believe," he said, twitching his consider-able nose over the rim of his glass, "that the Hollywood star world is an incestuous and narcissistic one. They wish to be seen and adored, and their friends are all simply status symbols, as are their cars, houses, and clothes with particular labels. Their world is made up, then, of those people and things with which they wish to be associated."

"Well, that pretty much disposes of them."

He ignored me. "Frazer Benson was one of those people with whom one wished to be associated. He had recently become a billionaire. He was both a financier and an extremely expensive consultant on investments."

"So what happened, he gave some bad advice and some-body got mad? Or some husband didn't appreciate Benson advising his wife in his bedroom?"

"Mr. Benson was at Jack Magnuson's birthday party just over a week ago. He was apparently a close friend of Mr. Magnuson's. While there, Mr. Benson apparently got into conversation with Melanie Westwood. She claimed he was drunk and, in her words, 'talked a lot of bullshit.' Shortly after that conversation, he left and went home, where he was murdered some time shortly after four a.m."

"You know the time because the security cameras on his gate recorded the time of his arrival."

"Correct."

"Sir, not that I don't enjoy your narrative style—in fact,

I was just thinking you really ought to be on the radio with that voice—but I have two questions. First, what makes this a federal case? Why are the Feds involved at all? And, more to the point, what makes it even remotely interesting for us?"

"That is three questions, Alex."

"Yes, sir. I'll boil it down to one. This is a simple murder investigation with no federal angle and no national security angle, so why are we interested?"

"Reserve your judgment until you have all the facts. You will fly to Los Angeles and pay a visit to Miss Westwood on Moraga Drive, in Bel-Air. Listen to her story. You may change your mind." He reached into his drawer, pulled out a small manila envelope, and dropped it in front of me. "You will be Special Agent Alex Mason. Your badge and other identification is in there. Take the company plane. If I am right, which of course I am, we do not want to be wasting time."

———

SOME TWO THOUSAND three hundred miles away, deep in a valley in Bel-Air, not a mile from the Getty View Park, a tall, thin man in a dark gray suit parked his anonymous, metallic gray Toyota Camry outside the large gate on Moraga Drive and walked to the video-entryphone, where he pressed call and looked up at the camera so it could see his face. It was a long, thin face.

A woman's voice answered, asking who he was. He pulled a Federal Bureau of Investigation badge from his inside pocket, opened it, held it up to be seen clearly by the camera, and enunciated, "Jeremiah Brown, Federal Bureau of Investigation. I'd like to ask Ms. Westwood a few questions. May I come in?"

There was a pause for maybe fifteen seconds, then the gate buzzed and opened. He looked up at the camera again, smiled and raised a hand in thanks, then walked in on long, thin legs.

He was met at the door by Isabel, who showed him through a large, terracotta-tiled entrance hall to a spacious living room with a bare, redbrick fireplace and low bookcases against every wall.

The voice made him start and turn. Melanie Westwood stood in jeans and a sweatshirt addressing her maid. "Isa, bring some lemonade, please." She stopped and smiled at the man. "Unless you would like something else."

He stared at her for a moment, smiling. His mouth was like a large V, she thought, into which his sharp nose fit perfectly. But his eyes, like two crescents, were an unnerving pale blue.

"No!" he said suddenly. "Lemonade, what could be better on a sunny day like this?"

She gestured to a chair. "Please, won't you sit?"

"Thank you." He sat, still staring at her with his mouth slightly open. "Forgive me, it must be tedious for you. I bet you hear it all the time. But I am a great admirer of your work. So versatile. I always think you must have such empathy to be able to understand such a wide variety of characters."

"Oh." He watched with pleasure as her cheeks colored. She spread her hands. "It's a craft. But I'm sure you didn't come here to talk about my work. How can I help you, Special Agent Brown?"

"I know you have been over this already, and I am sorry to burden you with more questions. The thing is, you see, we are conducting a separate investigation involving international trade, liquid assets, and money laundering." He waved his hand, suggesting it was all boring, complicated stuff. "But we have reason to believe Mr. Benson's death may be connected."

"I see. Well, by all means ask, but I am not sure I can tell you anything I didn't tell your colleagues."

Isabel came in with a large glass jug of bright yellow lemonade that clinked with ice. She placed it on the table beside Melanie and withdrew while Melanie filled two glasses. He rose, on his long, thin legs to take the glass she offered him.

"What I am really most interested in, Miss Westwood, is what, precisely, in as much detail as you can, Mr. Benson told you at the party."

She took a deep breath and gazed out of the window. Her bright red rosebushes were there, and she would really much rather have been tending to them than talking to this man, with his long, thin legs.

"He was pretty incoherent," she said. "He was talking about some club he belonged to in France. He said the members were all politicians, high-ranking European Union officials, judges, and billionaires."

"Did he say where in France?"

She thought for a moment. "I'm not sure. He said something about the region of Occitanie, Coudrey? South of Foix. He said the club was at a castle. He said the castle had an Occitan name rather than French." She paused to think. "Castèl de Coudrey? It was something like that."

The man chortled as he made notes. "The fantasies of some people. Did he say what kind of things they got up to at this club?"

"My impression at first was that he was trying to impress me. He made it sound like the Bilderberg Group or the Illuminati. They all got together to smoke cigars and drink cognac and manipulate international affairs."

"Anything specific or particular?"

She studied the man's face for a moment. It was something about his eyes. She shook her head.

"No. As I say, the impression I had at the time was that it was all bullshit. Frazer was fabulously rich, but he never got tired of telling you. He was a very insecure man who needed to boast and conquer all the time. He'd been hitting on me for a long time. I assumed that was what he was doing then. Trying to impress me. As I told your colleague, I only approached you because it was that same night..."

She trailed off. Agent Brown said, "That he was killed."

"Yes."

"You certainly did the right thing. It is probably as you say, just showing off, but because of his connections and the amount of money he made in the last couple of years, we have to look into it."

"Sure."

She sipped, and he watched her in silence. She drew breath to ask him if there was anything else, but he cut her short. "Many people like Mr. Benson are so foolish. A man in his position, carrying the responsibility of so much wealth, his responsibility to his clients, and his contacts, a man like that should not drink and boast. He should be modest and mature. And discreet. Do you not think so, Ms. Westwood?"

She didn't answer. He went on, "Take a woman of your own substantial wealth and achievement. So many people depend on you. Not just your employees, but friends and family. But you, you see, have the wisdom of your considerable intelligence and experience in life. And that makes you discreet."

She frowned and set down her half-empty glass. "I am not sure—"

"Indiscretion," he said as though she had not spoken. "Indiscretion costs lives, and what is worse, it costs pain. Pain to the indiscreet, to those who love them, and those they love."

"Special Agent Brown—"

"I mean," he said, setting down his glass, untouched, "look at the way poor Mr. Benson died. It is hard for most of us to imagine what he went through, but to a woman with such empathy as you have, it must be an awful thing to imagine. If only he had been discreet, it might never have happened."

He stood. He seemed very tall as she looked up at his thin, gray face and his pale eyes. She tried to speak, but fear had constricted her throat.

"Please, don't get up, I don't want to take your time. Time is so precious. I am sure it was just as you said. He was just showing off to a beautiful, desirable lady. I should just forget the whole thing if I were you."

"Yes," she said. "I—" Her mouth was dry, and she licked her lips. "I am sure you're right." She laughed. It was a strained, humorless laugh. "It was just a silly, drunken episode. It's fading from my mind as we speak."

"That's right, Ms Westwood. That's the ticket. Goodbye."

He turned and walked away on his long, thin legs, with his strange, almost loping stride. She heard the door close, rose, and hurried to the kitchen, where she and Isa watched him on the camera as he crossed the sidewalk to his car. The lights flashed, and he reached for the handle of the driver's door. There he paused, turned, and smiled straight at them. He opened the door, climbed in, and reversed away.

"Who was that man, *señora*? I don' like him."

She didn't answer but turned and made her way back to the living room, where she stood staring at her blood-red roses through the window.

"*Señora?*"

She turned and saw Isa in the door, holding a cloth too tightly with both hands. She gave a small, quiet laugh.

"It was nothing, Isa. Just a rather strange agent from the FBI." She looked back at the window and spoke half to herself. "If you hadn't seen him too, I might have thought I had dreamed it."

———

NOT A MILE AWAY, Lou was giggling in his car. He wished he had somebody he could phone and tell, but since his mother had died back at the turn of the millennium, he had had nobody to talk to or confide in. But that didn't mean he couldn't pretend. He hunched his shoulders and grinned.

"Beep beep beep, beep beep beep, beep beep, beep

beep." He paused a moment, still chuckling, then said, "Brrrp brrp, brrp brrrp, brr, '*Hello*?'" He used a high-pitched, squeaky voice for his mother. "Hi Mom, how was your day? '*Oh, you know, same as usual. My knee's been hurting. How about you, son?*' Well you'll never guess where *I've* just been, and who *I've* just been talking to! '*Well don't keep me in suspenders, son. I hope you haven't got yourself into trouble again!*' No, ma'am. I have just been talking to *Melanie Westwood*, in her own home in Bel-Air!"

He laughed long and loud, then drove in silence for a while. When he turned onto Sunset Boulevard he heaved a deep sigh. "I sure hope I don't have to kill her, Mom. I really like Melanie Westwood."

He lapsed into silence and by a roundabout route made his way through Beverly Hills and Mid City to South Broadway, where he left his Toyota at the gas station on the intersection with Slauson Avenue. There he pulled an unused burner from his pocket and dialed a number in France.

———

HUMBERTO DA SILVA was sitting down to have an early dinner. The table at the head of which he sat was large enough to accommodate twenty-four people with comfortable elbow room. The dining room, one of three in the Castèl de Coudrey, had a high ceiling supported on magnificent oak rafters, a fifteenth-century fireplace as big as a Manhattan apartment, and several coats of arms displayed on the walls.

Before him on the table was a classic vichyssoise which his chef, Diat, did exceptionally well, and waiting in the kitchen was a roasted suckling pig with apple sauce, another specialty of his master chef.

He tucked his crisp, white linen napkin into his waistcoat and raised his spoon, and his cell phone rang. He closed his eyes and shook his head.

"*Pourquoi?*" he asked quietly. "*Pourquoi maintenant?*" He picked up the cell. "*Oui?*"

The voice on the other end was quiet, soft, and yet oddly disagreeable.

"Oh, I'm not sure if I have the right number. Did your friend Tom order a steak and fries?"

Humberto grunted. He picked up his heavy, silver spoon and moved his soup about. "Tell me."

"The steak was delivered suitably deviled and seared, *pour encourager les autres*, as requested, and I just left the fries quivering in the pan. I am pretty sure there will be no need to go for another steak. The fries were appropriately encouraged."

"*Voila*, I am afraid you have the wrong number. I do not know this Tom of whom you speak."

"I apologize, *monsieur.*"

"*Bonne soirée.*"

He hung up and started in on his soup. So Frazer was dead, and Melanie Westwood had been silenced. He did not, as a rule, favor leaving potential witnesses alive, but this was a rare case. Two high-profile killings so close to each other in space and time would invite too much unwelcome attention. A good scare would do the job, and besides, if she were to speak to anyone, what would she tell, that Frazer Benson was a deluded conspiracy theorist? She would not give them any trouble. And if she did, well, in six months or a year, there would be an unfortunate boating accident, a fall while skiing, or a crash in a tunnel in Paris.

He chuckled as he spooned the last of his cold soup into his mouth and reached for the silver bell. He was ready now for the suckling pig.

Scan the QR code below to purchase BROTHERHOOD OF THE GOAT
Or go to: righthouse.com/brotherhood-of-the-goat

www.ingramcontent.com/pod-product-compliance
Lightning Source LLC
Chambersburg PA
CBHW030329200626
46816CB00006BA/1990